LET'S READ MORE STORIES

Let's Read More Stories

Selected by SIDONIE MATSNER GRUENBERG

ILLUSTRATED BY DAGMAR WILSON

Garden City Books
GARDEN CITY, NEW YORK

ACKNOWLEDGMENTS

The editor and publisher express grateful appreciation for the use of material listed below:

"A B C of Wheels" by Eve Merriam. Copyright, ©, 1960, by Doubleday & Company, Inc. Courtesy of the author.

"Bertram Goes to the Moon" by Paul T. Gilbert. Copyright, 1952, 1953, by *Child Life*. Courtesy of Mrs. Ilse F. Gilbert.

"The Bottle that Went to Sea" by Lilian Moore. Copyright, 1955, by Humpty Dumpty, Inc. Courtesy of the author.

"Cherry Stones" by A. A. Milne from the book, *Now We Are Six*. Copyright, 1927, by E. P. Dutton & Co., Inc. Renewal, 1955, by A. A. Milne. Courtesy of the publishers.

"Easter Treat." by Roger Duvoisin. Copyright, 1954, by Alfred A. Knopf, Inc. Courtesy of the publishers.

"Eddie Goes to Dancing School" by Carolyn Haywood from the book, *Eddie and the Fire Engine*. Copyright, 1949, by William Morrow and Company, Inc. Courtesy of the publishers.

"Guess What's in the Grass" by Lucy Sprague Mitchell from the book, *Believe and Make-Believe,* edited by Lucy Sprague Mitchell and Irma Simonton Black. Copyright, 1956, by the Bank Street College of Education. Courtesy of the publishers, E. P. Dutton & Co., Inc.

"Helping Hilda" by Emma Brock from *Kristie and the Colt and the Others*. Copyright, 1949, by Alfred A. Knopf, Inc. Courtesy of the publishers.

"How Gerald Caught a Filla-Ma-Zokk" by Dr. Seuss. Copyright, 1954, by *Children's Activities*. Courtesy of the author and MCA Management, Ltd.

"The Lamby-Sitter" by Lee Kingman. Copyright, 1954, by Story-a-Day, Inc. Courtesy of the author.

"Lights" by Claudia Lewis. Copyright, ©, 1960, by Doubleday & Company, Inc. Courtesy of the author.

"Loopy" by Hardie Gramatky. Copyright, 1941, by Hardie Gramatky. Courtesy of the publishers, G. P. Putnam's Sons.

"The Lucky Number" by Catherine Woolley. Copyright, 1953, by Story-a-Day, Inc. Courtesy of the author.

"Meow!" by Eva Grant. Copyright, ©, 1960, by Doubleday & Company, Inc. Courtesy of the author.

"Mr. Scrunch" by Alf Evers. Copyright, 1939, by *Child Life*. Courtesy of the author.

"Mrs. Moodle and the Tea-Tray" by Rose Fyleman from *Forty Good Morning Tales*. Copyright, 1929, by Doubleday & Company, Inc. Courtesy of the publishers, Doubleday & Company, Inc. (New York) and Methuen & Co. Ltd. (London).

"My Mother is the Most Beautiful Woman in the World" by Becky Reyher. Copyright, 1945, by Becky Reyher and Ruth Gannett. Courtesy of the publishers, Lothrop, Lee and Shepard Co.

"A Nickel for a Pickle" by Rosalie Lowell. Copyright, ©, 1960, by Doubleday & Company, Inc. Courtesy of the author.

"Nino and His Fish" by Edith Thacher Hurd and Clement Hurd. Copyright, 1954, by Edith Thacher Hurd and Clement Hurd. Courtesy of the publishers, Lothrop, Lee and Shepard Co., Inc.

"The Pasture" by Robert Frost from *Complete Poems of Robert Frost*. Copyright, 1930, 1949, by Henry Holt and Company, Inc. Courtesy of the publishers.

"Pancho" by Berta and Elmer Hader. Copyright, 1942, by Berta Hader and Elmer Hader. Courtesy of The Macmillan Company, publishers.

"The Penny Puppy" by Robert Garfield from *The Penny Puppy and Other Dog Stories*. Copyright, 1949, by Simon and Schuster, Inc., and Artists and Writers Guild, Inc. Courtesy of the publishers.

"Pick Me Up" by William Jay Smith from *Laughing Time*. Copyright, 1955, by William Jay Smith. Courtesy of Little Brown & Company, the publishers.

"The Story of the Teasing Monkey" by Helen Bannerman. Courtesy of James Nisbet and Company, Ltd. (Hertfordshire, England), Dr. Davie A. D. Bannerman, Executor of Estate of Helen Bannerman, and J. B. Lippincott Company (U.S.A.).

"Stripes and Spots" by Dahlov Ipcar. Copyright, 1953, by Dahlov Ipcar. Appeared originally in *Child Life*. Courtesy of the author.

"Trees" by Harry Behn, from *The Little Hill*. Copyright, 1949, by Harry Behn. Courtesy of the publishers, Harcourt, Brace and Company, Inc.

"That Rapscallion Cat, Sneakers" by Margaret Wise Brown, from the book *Sneakers*. Copyright, 1955, by Estate of Margaret Wise Brown. Courtesy of the publishers, William R. Scott, Inc.

"The Magic Whistle" by Adèle and Cateau De Leeuw. Copyright, 1953, by Adèle and Cateau De Leeuw. Courtesy of the authors.

"What Would You Do, If . . ." by Leonore Klein. Copyright, 1956, by Leonore Klein. Courtesy of the publishers, William R. Scott, Inc.

"The White Horse" by Alice Dalgliesh, from *Jack and Jill*. Copyright, 1938, by The Curtis Publishing Company. Courtesy of the author.

"Why Cowboys Sing in Texas" by Le Grand Henderson. Copyright, 1950, by Abingdon Press. Courtesy of the publishers.

The editor is very grateful to her colleague, Bella Koral, for her skillful help and counsel in the selection of these stories.

For JOEL WILLIAM and MATTHEW ALAN,
the youngest of our eleven grandchildren.

Dear Boys and Girls:

So many of you have liked the stories and verses in my book LET'S READ A STORY that I was very happy to find more stories and verses that I felt you would like as well. That's why I call this collection LET'S READ MORE STORIES. And those of you who see this book first may want to read the other one too.

Here we have stories about real boys and girls, some of whom had exciting adventures—like the boy who captured a bull, or the one who had lots of fun planning a trip to the moon before anybody had sent a rocket up so far. Or the girl who was very eager to be a baby sitter and found a way to become a very expert one.

And you will find stories about animals, like the one about the mischievous cat, or the one about the stripey tiger, or the one about the teasing monkey.

And of course we have stories of fun and fancy, like the one about the magic whistle, or the puzzling story about IF, or the story of singing cowboys.

I hope that hearing these stories and verses read to you will bring you many hours of fun. Before very long, you will have fun reading them to yourself. Then you will want to go on reading many more stories of many different kinds, about all sorts of people in all parts of the world, and stories about animals and stars and mountains and seas. And also stories about long ago and stories about what never happened at all!

SIDONIE MATSNER GRUENBERG

Contents

LET'S READ MORE STORIES

The Penny Puppy

BY ROBERT GARFIELD

Once there was a small puppy, just the color of a bright new penny. He had a shiny coat, a merry bark, and a smiling face, but he belonged to nobody at all. When he was sleepy, he slept wherever he happened to be. When he was hungry, he chewed small bones that the big dogs wouldn't bother with. When he was thirsty, he drank out of little puddles left by the rain.

It was not a bad life for a stray little puppy.

But one day, this little puppy saw another little puppy trotting along, head high, tail held gaily, at the heels of a small boy. The boy took three steps, and stopped to pet the puppy. He skipped three skips, and stopped to talk to the puppy.

The stray puppy watched them, with his head cocked to one side.

"I'd like to belong to a boy, too," he said to himself.

He jumped up and ran after the other puppy. But when the other puppy saw him, it growled.

"This is *my* boy," it said, showing all its sharp little teeth.

The stray puppy backed away.

"So that's the way it is," he thought. "Well, then, I'll just find a boy of my own."

And away he went, up the hill, looking all around for a boy with no puppy.

He saw lots of boys.

He saw a snub-nosed boy with a big fluffy puppy, so fluffy it was hard to tell which end was the front. And he saw a tow-headed boy with a tiny sleek puppy.

He saw a boy throwing a ball to a barking puppy, and a boy giving a bone to a dancing puppy.

And then, all at once, he saw a boy all alone, with no puppy at all.

"There's the boy I want!" barked the stray puppy, and he scrambled toward the corner where the boy was standing.

But a bicycle whizzed in front of him. . . .

And a big foot almost stepped on him. . . .

And a pushcart rolled past him, barely missing his little tail.

By the time that puppy got to the corner, the boy was just climbing into a trolley that was in a hurry to go.

"Wait!" barked the puppy.

The little boy heard him. He looked back, and he looked as if he wanted to come back. But it was too late. The door slammed shut, the bell clanged, and away went the trolley, banging and swinging up the hill.

The puppy ran after it. He ran until his paws were hot and his mouth was full of dust.

He barked "Wait for me!" and "Come back!" and then a

disappointed "BOW-wow-wow!" for now the trolley was disappearing over the top of a hill.

The puppy stopped running.

He jumped up the high curb, and sat on the hot sidewalk on the hot hill, right in the middle of the hot town, panting and looking all around.

He saw a drugstore and a shoe store and an ice-cream store. He saw a store with a window full of puppies of all kinds. He trotted over and sat down in front of that store.

He watched a lady go in with no dog. When she came out, she had a proud, white poodle trotting at her side.

He saw a man go in with a frown and come out with a brown bulldog under his arm, and a big smile on his face.

"That's the place for me," thought the stray little puppy.

He put up his tail and his ears and ran through the open door. He ran straight to the storekeeper, stood up, and grinned.

But the storekeeper shook his head.

"I'm sorry, puppy," he said. "I have too many puppies. I can't feed even one more."

Then all the dogs and puppies in the store began to growl. "Go away, puppy! We were here first!"

The puppy scooted out the door. He sat down sadly in the shade of an awning.

Now a fat, jolly balloon man came walking up the street.

"Balloons," the man called. "Balloons! Who'll buy my nice-a ten-cent balloons!"

But nobody wanted any balloons.

"Bad day for selling my balloons," muttered the balloon man. He wiped his forehead and stopped to rest. And then he saw the stray little puppy near his feet.

"What's-a the matter, puppy?" he asked. "You have-a no home?"

The puppy barked to say, no, he didn't. He said it was a bad day for puppies, too. And he looked so small and so wistful that the balloon man picked him up in his big hand.

"You look-a tired," he said. "You look-a hungry. Lonesome, too!"

He tucked the stray little puppy in his big pocket, and strolled on down the hill.

"I'll sell-a my balloons," he told the puppy. "Then we'll go to my house and have a good supper."

The puppy thought about the boy on the trolley. He wanted to be the boy's puppy. But the balloon man's pocket was soft and cozy, and his voice sounded buzzy and drowsy. Before long the tired little puppy fell fast asleep.

The balloon man walked slowly up and down the hot streets.

"Balloons," he called. "Balloons! Who'll buy my nice-a ten-cent balloons?"

But nobody would buy a balloon.

"Maybe these balloons cost-a too much," thought the balloon man. "I'll change-a the price."

He called, "Balloons! Five-a cents apiece!" And people came running out of their houses.

And a little boy bought a red balloon.

And a little girl bought a green balloon.

An uncle bought two yellow balloons for his twin nephews, and a grandmother bought ten balloons of different colors for her ten grandchildren.

Now the balloon man had only two balloons left, but he was hotter than ever, and very thirsty. He counted all his money. It was enough to buy supper for a fat balloon man and a small puppy.

"I walk-a down one more street," said the balloon man. "If I can't sell-a these two balloons, I just let them go up, up, up in the air where it's nice and cool."

And down the street he went, very slowly, because his feet were so hot.

He called, "Balloons!" and it sounded soft and fuzzy in the

hot afternoon.

"Nice-a balloons," sang the balloon man. "Only five-a cents for two."

But nobody wanted those balloons.

The balloon man was just about to let them go up, up, up, when he saw a little boy swinging on a gate.

"You like-a balloons?" he asked. "Two for what you want to pay."

The little boy looked at those fine balloons. He looked at the red one, and he looked at the blue one. And he took a bright new penny out of his pocket.

He looked and looked at that penny.

"They're very nice balloons," he said. "But I think I'll keep this penny to buy a puppy like the little puppy that ran after me when I was riding on the trolley."

The balloon man smiled a jolly smile.

He winked to himself, put his big hand into his big pocket—and brought out the penny-colored puppy.

"You like-a puppy like this?" he asked.

The little boy stared at the sleeping puppy.

"Just like that," he whispered. "That's the very *same* puppy that I saw uptown!"

The balloon man stroked the puppy's head. The puppy woke up, and when he saw the little boy, he wagged his tail until he wriggled all over. He smiled until his eyes closed into slanting slits.

"It's the *same* little boy who went off in the trolley," he barked merrily.

The boy held out his penny and looked up at the balloon man.

"Can I buy him for a penny?" he asked.

The balloon man shook his head.

"No, sir!" he said. "You don't have-a to buy this puppy at all. I think he's-a *your* puppy!"

Then the little boy reached out his arms, and the puppy jumped right into them.

And down the street went the balloon man, calling, "Balloons, balloons, who buy-a my balloons?"

He sounded so tired that the little boy ran after him, with the puppy at his heels.

"I'll buy them," he said, and he gave the balloon man his bright new penny.

He took the red balloon for himself, and the blue one for his puppy, and he skipped back toward his house.

Every three steps he stopped to pet his new puppy, or to talk to him. And the little puppy was so happy that he barked and grinned and almost lost his balloon a dozen times.

The balloon man was happy, too.

"I sold-a two balloons at once!" he chuckled to himself, "and I don't have a hungry puppy to feed!"

He started back toward the ice-cream store.

"I'll get-a nice cold ice-cream cone," he said. "Then I'll go go home. Tomorrow I sell-a more balloons—maybe more-a puppies, too!"

The Pasture

BY ROBERT FROST

I'm going out to clean the pasture spring;
I'll only stop to rake the leaves away
(And wait to watch the water clear, I may):
I sha'n't be gone long.—You come too.

I'm going out to fetch the little calf
That's standing by the mother. It's so young,
It totters when she licks it with her tongue.
I sha'n't be gone long.—You come too.

Helping Hilda

BY EMMA L. BROCK

Hilda was the most helping child on the banks of the Father of Waters. She began helping when she slid from her bed in the morning. She helped all through the live-long day and stopped only when she climbed into bed at night.

She helped her mother and her father in their home in the city. Now that she was visiting Aunt Selma in Little River, she was helping her, too.

She could make beds without losing the blankets on the floor more than once or twice. She could dust the chairs and the tables and leave most of the vases on the bookcases. She wiped only a few handles from the cups and she could carry a bag of groceries along the village street without spilling more than one or two things. She was a great help to everyone.

"Are you coming with me to buy the groceries, Hilda?" Aunt Selma asked one day. "When we come back I will make gingerbread."

"Oh, goodie!" shouted Hilda. "Gingerbread! I like that just about more than chocolate cake. Can I help make it?"

"Why, yes," said Aunt Selma. "There are some things you could do to help."

Hilda had an idea.

"I think I will stay at home and do the dusting. Then I'll be ready to help with the gingerbread."

Aunt Selma looked a little surprised, because Hilda liked to go shopping better than anything else.

"Oh, all right, Hilda. There will not be much to carry home. I can easily do it." Aunt Selma put her bag over her arm and walked toward Main Street where the grocery was.

Hilda danced a jig in the middle of the living room and tossed her dusting mitt in the air.

"I'll just hurry and finish this and then——"

She swished here and she swushed there. A book fell on the floor, but the vases only rocked around some. Swish, swush. All the time she was singing under her breath: "Gingerbread, gingerbread, molasses and brown sugar, eggs and milk and flour and eggs and sugar, molasses and ginger, ginger, ginger! Oh, yum, yum, yum!"

"There, that will do," sang Hilda, as she tossed the dusting mitt into the closet and skipped into the kitchen.

She tied on Aunt Selma's apron that came down to her feet.

"I will just get out all the things to make the gingerbread. What a help it will be!"

"Milk," said Hilda.

She carried the milk from the refrigerator.

"Lard," said Hilda. "Butter, maybe," and she put them on the table.

"Ginger."

She opened the can of ginger and sniffed a hard sniff, such a hard sniff that her nose tickled.

"Eggs next," she said.

She took out some eggs and held them in her hands. She held them in her hands while she wriggled her nose all around and up and down to keep from sneezing. It was the ginger sneeze.

"Atch, atch, atch," cried Hilda. "Atch, atch, atch, CHEW!"

The sneeze shook Hilda all over. It shook her head. It twitched her hair. It shook her shoulders and her arms. It twitched her hands. And away flew one of the eggs. Sklutch! Down on the floor!

"Oh, dear," said Hilda. "It broke. It broke all in pieces. I'll have to pick it up."

Hilda put the other eggs carefully on the table and bent over. It was easy to pick up the shell, but the lump of white and yellow slid away. She tried to scoop it up with a spoon. The egg slipped this way and that. Her fingers could not push it into the spoon.

Slowly Hilda backed away as the egg slid over the floor. Hilda backed away, and the egg slid after her. It slid from the refrigerator to the table to the sink, and to the back door. It left a long slippery streak behind it. It grew smaller and smaller until there was only a little blob of it left.

Hilda looked at it and sighed.

"Guess I'll just have to scrub the floor," she said.

And she did. She sloshed it, and she scrubbed it, and she wiped it. She scrubbed until the egg was all washed away.

"There. That will help Aunt Selma," said Hilda, as she wrung out the scrubbing rag and pushed some wet hair back from her forehead. "She won't have to scrub the floor. Now the molasses."

Hilda carried the molasses bottle to the table and tried to turn the top. She jerked and twisted.

"It's stuck!" said Hilda.

Just then Nils Nilsson came across the kitchen. He was Aunt

Selma's white cat. Nils Nilsson mewed and rubbed against Hilda's legs.

She jerked at the bottle top. She jerked and twisted. And flip! Off the top came. The bottle rocked on the table. Then over it went, and the molasses began to run. A thick sticky stream ran over the table and down on the floor. It ran over Nils Nilsson's feet, the sticky brown molasses.

Nils Nilsson did not like molasses. He did not like to eat it and he liked it even less on his feet. He jumped high in the air and then skipped across the kitchen. Quick as a wink he climbed up the kitchen curtains and down again. Then he hid behind the stove.

Hilda stood with her hands in the air as the drops of molasses flew from the feet of Nils Nilsson all over and up and down. All around on the floor, all over the curtains, all over the stove!

"Nils!" she cried. "Why, Nils, Nils! There is molasses on

everything. Come let me wash you, before you do any more."

She pulled Nils from under the stove and carried him to the sink. She scrubbed his feet with the scrubbing rag as well as she could. Nils wriggled so fast that she was not sure which foot she had just washed, but she did eight of them as well as she could. Then she put him out the back door.

"I think I had better scrub the floor again," said Hilda.

And she did. She scrubbed up all the sticky spots that she could find. She washed the bottoms of her shoes and the top of the table. She wiped the molasses bottle all around.

"I'll have to wash the curtains too, I guess, and Aunt Selma's apron," and she put them to soak in a pan of water. "Aunt Selma will be glad to have this done for her. The curtains and the apron will be clean. Perhaps I could iron them too. Where did the top of the molasses bottle go?"

"Hello there," and in walked Aunt Selma, back from her marketing. "Oh, you've been helping!"

"Yes," said Hilda, and she crawled out from under the sink with the top of the molasses bottle clutched in her hand. Her face was red. There was a streak of molasses across her chin.

"Yes," she said, as she wiped the bottle top with the scrubbing rag. "I've been getting things ready for the gingerbread. And cleaning up a little too. The egg and the molasses, you know. I've scrubbed Nils and the kitchen floor. Two times I scrubbed the floor. Perhaps you had better iron the curtains, because my ironing is wobbly, but I did the rest. Don't you think I am a big help to you, Aunt Selma?"

Aunt Selma was very busy getting out the gingerbread recipe.

"Oh, Hilda," she cried, and she was laughing. "You are the helpingest girl in this whole wide country. I don't know what I would do without you!"

Hilda was pulling her foot from a sticky place on the floor.

"I'm so glad, Aunt Selma," she said.

"Now what more can I do to help?"

That Rapscallion Cat, Sneakers

BY MARGARET WISE BROWN

Once there was a little fat cat, and his name was Sneakers.

His mother called him Sneakers, because he had four white paws and the rest of him was inky black.

All her other kittens were inky black all over.

The first time that his mother saw Sneakers lying with his four white paws waving in the air, she thought he must have gone wading in her saucer of milk.

She picked him out of her pile of kittens by the scruff of his neck.

Then she lay down and held him, squirming between her two front paws, while she tried to clean the milk off his tiny white feet and make them inky black like all her other kittens' feet.

She licked and she licked and she purred a song while she licked.

But the milk would not come off!

And she licked and she licked, and she purred and she purred, but still he had four white paws.

Just then the mother cat saw the little boy running toward her.

It was the first warm day in the year, and he had on a pair of brand-new, clean white sneakers.

The mother cat looked at the little boy's sneakers.

And she blinked at her kitten with its four white paws.

And then she purred and she purred and she purred.

And the little kitten was called Sneakers from then on.

Now Sneakers was a rapscallion cat from the time he was born.

The other kittens stayed in the box until they grew up enough.

But Sneakers was off even before he grew up enough.

Sneakers went off after little black bugs.

He chased butterfly shadows across the ground.

He pounced on people's shoelaces if they were the least bit hanging.

Sneakers went *pounce, pounce, pounce,* all day long.

And then he went *pounce* into his bed at night.

And, curling his little white feet under him into a warm fur ball, he went *pounce* to sleep.

His mother always knew that, no matter how much he went pouncing off, he would always come pouncing back, so she didn't worry about him.

But she did think, over and over again, "By the incredible velvet that grows on my nose, this is a funny little cat!"

One day his mother licked his little face all clean and smooth.

And she said, "Now Sneakers, my kitten, my little fur cat, away you go!"

"You are to live in the house with the little boy, and make him laugh, and chase away the mice, and never knock anything off the tables."

"I am a barn cat, and my home is here, in the barn in the hay."

"But you will be a house cat, and you will sleep before the fire and only come out here in the daytime."

"Now off you go to the house, and keep your little paws clean as the milk you drink every morning."

So off Sneakers went to live in the big house and be the little boy's kitten.

At first, it seemed very quiet in the house at night after the barn.

Sneakers missed the sound of the horses stomping in their stalls and the mice squeaking and squealing in the hayloft.

Then, at table one day, purely by accident, the little boy knocked over a plate of peaches.

They rolled all over the floor in every direction—little round peaches rolling away.

"My, but I'm glad this happened," thought the funny little kitten.

And he batted one of the peaches around on the floor.

"I do wish that lots of things would come spilling all over the floor for me to chase every day."

Everyone laughed so hard to see Sneakers scooting around after the peaches with his paw they forgot who knocked the peaches over.

The little boy laughed, too.

But the little kitten never knocked things off himself.

He just prowled round and round with one eye cocked and waited for things to happen.

One afternoon the cook came back from town all dressed up in a brand-new hat—a brand-new hat with red feathers on it.

She met Sneakers in the pantry.

"Where are you going, you little Sneaker Cat?" she said to him.

"Just *prowling around, prowling around,*" answered Sneakers.

(Or at least that's what it sounded like, as he purred and blinked his bright yellow eyes.)

Whiff! The wind came blowing in at the kitchen door.

It blew the cook's hat off with all its red feathers.

Pounce went Sneakers!

Pounce on the feathers and the brand-new hat.

And he slid across the floor.

"Oh, Sneakers, you kitten, you rapscallion cat!"

"Give me back my brand-new hat!"

But Sneakers was having fun, and he knew the cook moved slowly.

He batted the hat with his paw.

"My, but I'm glad this happened!" he thought.

And he skidded the hat under the table.

The cook had to chase Sneakers all over the kitchen and into the sink before she could get her brand-new hat.

She put it back on her head—right on top of her head.

And she stood there, looking at Sneakers.

Sneakers just sat by the side of the sink—where he wasn't supposed to be—and licked his milk-white paws.

"Oh, Sneakers," said the cook, "the minute I saw you, I knew you were in here just waiting to get into some kind of mischief."

"No," said Sneakers, "I was just *prowling around, prowling around.*"

(Or that is what he seemed to be saying.)

And he walked out of the kitchen on his four white paws to find the little boy.

The little boy was at the barn, making the harness soft and clean with saddle soap and a wet sponge.

"Hello, Sneaker Cat," said the little boy. "Where are you going?"

"Just *prowling around, prowling around,*" said Sneakers.

And he rubbed his fur back against the little boy's bare leg.

Then he sat down to wait for something to happen—for the sponge to drop, or something to spill.

For Sneakers was a rapscallion cat.

Cherry Stones

BY A. A. MILNE

Tinker, Tailor, Soldier, Sailor,
Rich Man, Poor Man, Ploughboy, Thief—

And what about a Cowboy,
Policeman, Jailer,
Engine-driver,
Or Pirate Chief?
What about a Postman—or a Keeper at the Zoo?
What about the Circus Man who lets the people through?
And the man who takes the pennies for the roundabouts and swings,
Or the man who plays the organ, and the other man who sings?
What about the Conjuror with rabbits in his pockets?
What about a Rocket Man who's always making rockets?

Oh, there's such a lot of things to do and such a lot to be
That there's always lots of cherries on my little cherry tree!

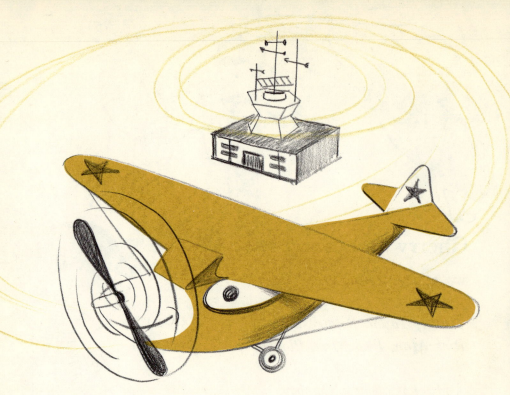

Loopy

BY HARDIE GRAMATKY

Loopy is a small airplane—the kind that flyers cheerfully called a hedgehopper.

That's because such a light, gay little plane can skim over the ground with the ease of a bird.

But even hedgehopping is a lot harder than it looks. One mistake and the ground feels very hard indeed.

Loopy had a healthy respect for the ground. Besides, he could not afford to make mistakes, for his job was to help the pilot teach flyers how to fly.

All day long he had to circle the airport, in an endless merry-go-round, while the students practiced on him.

And sometimes—at least until the beginners got used to being off the ground—it was pretty scary.

With the pilot steering him one minute, the student the next, poor Loopy had nothing to say about what was happening to him.

He never knew what to expect.

Except that, when a particularly clumsy fellow was learning, Loopy always expected the worst. . . .

. . . And often got it. When that happened the mechanics had to patch him together, and sometimes he was in the shop for days before he could go up again.

This was all very dull, and to pass the time Loopy would imagine what it would be like to fly by himself, with no pilot to hold him in check and no heavy-handed student to horse him around.

He could see himself indulging in some fancy skywriting which was what he really wanted to do.

. . . And even showing the birds themselves some real flying . . .

But all this was only a dream. Had it not been for a stroke of luck—which turned out to be as good in the end as it promised to be bad in the beginning—Loopy might have remained a patient, forgotten little drudge.

One day a show-off, a regular know-it-all, came out to the airport and persuaded the pilot to let him go up alone.

Loopy knew the type well. They always meant a bad afternoon.

And this particular afternoon, Loopy grimly decided, might be just *too bad*. For the show-off paid no attention to Loopy or what was going on in the sky. He had his greedy eyes glued on the crowd at the field until they disappeared from view.

This objectionable fellow didn't care anything about flying properly. He just wanted to show off.

Not so Loopy, who kept a weather eye cocked on the sky. Off in the distance he saw a big black cloud getting bigger and fatter all the time. The show-off, however, kept right on with his ridiculous antics.

Loopy coughed his motor and did everything he could
think of to warn the show-off of the danger ahead.

But
it
was
no
use.

Even the swirling winds on the very edge of the cloud made
no impression.

Suddenly they were inside, and it was black as night.

The wind blew like a hurricane.

Even with the propeller spinning like mad, Loopy could
make no headway. The winds rushed past, with the roar of an
express train, but

he
didn't
move.
He
just
stood
still.

And in his face the lightning flashed as it never does on
earth.

It scared the know-it-all out of his wits.

The dials on the instrument board glared back at him like
angry faces.

The know-it-all, if he knew nothing else, at least knew when
he had had enough. To get out of that angry, storm-tossed
cloud, he cowardly took to his parachute.

And there was poor Loopy, harried by wind and dark and
lightning, with no one to help him.

In the first moment he was as helpless as a blown-out
umbrella.

He felt himself falling—and as he fell he remembered the

things he had planned to do if he ever was on his own. Instinctively he worked his elevators and suddenly realized he could check his fall.

One more push and he was going up again—right over a mountain top.

Then, like a frightened trout giving a flip of the tail, he wiggled the rudder . . .

. . . And found—none too soon for him—that he could turn.

And when he finally tried his ailerons—those little movable parts of the wing—Loopy knew for sure what he had always believed: that he could really fly by himself. He could turn and bank and go up and down as he wished.

The storm no longer frightened him.

This was what he had always wanted to do. Completely confident now, he flashed in a distainful circle around the dangling parachutist . . .

This was great fun. If the gas had only held out, he would have kept it up all day. But Loopy, wise airman that he was, knew it was time to go home.

And everyone agreed it was one of the prettiest landings ever seen.

The crowd cheered and took pictures and pressed around the little plane. And the few who noticed the know-it-all when he came drifting down gave him the hoots and jeers he richly deserved.

It was the making of Loopy. Now he never bothers with students. He is a skywriter, the most famous of them all. And from the ground you can always tell his work by the smooth, clear letters and from the fact he never fails to dot his *i*'s.

The Story of the Teasing Monkey

BY HELEN BANNERMAN

Once upon a time there was a very mischievous little monkey, who lived in a big banyan tree, and his name was Jacko.

And in the jungle below there lived a huge, fierce old lion and lioness.

Now Jacko was a very teasing monkey. He used to climb down the long trailing roots of the banyan tree, and pull the tails of all the other creatures, and then scamper up again, before they could catch him.

And he was so bold, he even pulled the tails of the lion and lioness one day.

This made them so angry that——

They went to a grim old bear they knew, and they arranged

with him that he should come with them to the banyan tree, when Jacko was away.

So he came, and standing on the lion's head, he gnawed the roots through till they were so thin they would not bear a jerk.

And next time Jacko pulled the lion's tail he gave a great tug —the roots broke, and down fell Jacko, into the huge, fierce grim old lion's jaws! !

"Come here, my dear!" roared the lion.

The lioness came and looked at Jacko. "He is a very thin monkey," said she; "we had better put him in the larder for a week to fatten him, and then ask Mr. Bear to dinner."

So they put him in the larder, which was just a little piece at the end of their cave, built up with big stones, and while the lion built it up, the lioness lay ready to spring on him if he tried to escape. It was very dark and very cold, and Jacko did not like it at all.

They left a little window to feed him by, and every day they gave him as many bananas as he liked, because they knew monkeys ate bananas, and they could get them easily.

Then the lioness wrote a leaf-letter to the bear, asking him to dinner, which he, of course, accepted with pleasure.

But Jacko did not get fat, and the reason of that was that he soon tired of bananas, and only ate one every day. He gave all the others to the rats.

The lion and lioness were rather worried because Jacko did not get fat, so one day they stole in to listen to him talking to the rats, and as it happened they were just talking about bananas.

"I am tired of bananas," said Jacko. "I wish I could get a coconut."

"It would make you very fat," said the rats.

"Yes," said Jacko, "and I don't want to be fat for those old lions."

"Ho, ho!" said the lions. "A coconut will make him fat;

we'll get him one at once."

But when they came to the tree they could not reach a single coconut!

So the lion went back and told the little rats *very fiercely* that he would tear down the stones, and eat them all up at once, if they did not fetch him down some coconuts at once.

This terrified the little rats. They scampered up the tree, and gnawed off the coconuts as fast as they ever could.

But as the coconuts fell on the heads of the lion and lioness, and hurt them very much, the little rats took care to stay up the tree till it was dark.

As soon as their heads felt a little better, the lion and lioness took the coconuts.

And carried them to Jacko.

They had to make a very large hole to put them in, but they built it up carefully again.

Jacko was very much delighted to get the coconut, but he had hard work tearing off the hairy outside.

However at last he got it all off. Then he smashed the coconuts with a stone, and drank the milk, and began eating the nut; and wasn't it good after a whole week of bananas!

While he ate it he amused himself making a nice warm coat for himself of the hairy husk of the coconuts, and he was so busy he did not notice how much he was eating.

And when he put his warm coat on he just looked fearfully fat.

And the lion and lioness peeping in, thought it was all Jacko, and they were delighted.

"Isn't he fat and tender?" they said. "We'll eat him tonight, and not wait for Mr. Bear."

And they went out for a walk, to get a good appetite.

Poor Jacko! He did not eat any more coconut after he heard that. He pulled off his coat, and smoothed his hair down with his little paws, but still he looked fat.

And he smeared himself all over with bananas to make the hair lie flat, but *still* he looked fat.

So he put on his warm coat again, and lay down, and cried himself to sleep.

But you must know the bear was a very greedy old bear, and that very afternoon, while Jacko was asleep, he came to have a private peep at him.

And when he saw him looking so lovely and fat, he just could not resist the temptation, and began pulling down the stones as fast as he could, intending to eat him all by himself. But he was an awkward, clumsy old bear, and all of a sudden——— With a rumble and a *rattle* and a CLATTER, and a

CRASH!!!

the stones all came down on top of him, waking poor little Jacko, and scaring him nearly out of his wits. But he had the sense to scramble out as fast as he could.

The lion and lioness were just coming back, and when they heard the noise they came tearing home like the wind, and met little Jacko just in the mouth of the cave.

With a fearful roar the lion struck at him with his claws, but they only stuck in the—coconut coat.

Jacko wriggled out of it and ran on.

With another fearful roar, the lioness seized him in her teeth.

But Jacko was so round with eating coconut, and so slippery with banana, that he popped out from between her teeth, like an orange seed, and ran on.

And the next minute he was safe, and scrambling up the coconut tree at a rate which shook down most of the coconuts onto the heads of the lion and lioness.

So the lion had a sore head, and the lioness had a sore head, and the bear had a sore head, and they had nothing for dinner but

BANANAS!

Guess What's in the Grass

BY LUCY SPRAGUE MITCHELL

Something lay in the grass.

The wind blew over it and the grass went swish, swish round it. Once in a while this something in the grass moved. What was it?

All the animals wanted to find out.

A little field mouse crept through the grass. Her little feet made no sound. She slipped in and out through the leaves of the high grass. Her little mouse whiskers moved all the time. Nearer and nearer she crept toward what lay in the grass.

The little mouse lifted her head and peeped through the grass. Her little heart went very fast. Her little nose twitched. Right in front of her lay something. What was it? She stopped. She sniffed the thing all over. "I know what it is," thought the little mouse. "It is just something made of leather. I can smell it with my sharp nose." And she crept away through the grass, her little mouse whiskers moving all the time.

A great bird sailed high in the air. His wings were spread wide. Far, far below him lay a hump in the grass. What was it? He wanted to know. The great bird floated in the sky. Still, still he hung there, his great wings flapping in the wind. He was watching. The wind parted the leaves of grass a little over the middle of the hump in the grass. "I know what it is," thought the great bird. "It is just a shirt and some trousers. I can see them with my sharp eyes." And away sailed the bird through the sky.

A gray squirrel peeped out of her hole in a tree. She, too, wanted to find out what it was that lay in the grass.

Down below, the shirt in the grass moved and something stuck up out of the grass.

The squirrel jumped onto a branch of the tree. She held her tail up over her head. Then she stayed still with her head on one side. She was listening.

"Chee, chee, chee," chattered the squirrel. "I know what it is. I can hear it with my sharp ears. I can hear some little animal moving under that heap of clothes. The animal has a pink claw with five long pink things on the end." And the squirrel with her feathery tail went back into her hole in the tree.

A mother rabbit went hop, hop, through the grass. Her five babies lay warm in their grass nest, curled up like little balls of fur. The mother rabbit stood up on her back legs. She nibbled the sweet tops of the leaves of grass. Suddenly the mother rabbit stood still. Through her four paws she felt the earth tremble a little. Nearby, something in the grass rolled over. What was it? "I know what it is," thought the rabbit. "It is a big animal under the clothes. Through my paws I can feel the earth tremble when the animal rolls over." And the mother rabbit went hop, hop through the grass back to her babies.

A little mosquito came flying near by. He was singing his

mosquito song, "Z-z-z-z-z-z!" He flew down and lighted on something that was sticking up through the grass. He took a bite of it. Then another bite. "What a fine taste!" thought the mosquito. "Only noses taste like that. I want another bite." Just as the mosquito was taking another bite, he heard something. He lifted his head, and watched and listened. He saw something very big. It was a tall lady. And the mosquito flew away, very fast.

The tall lady came walking through the grass. She was looking all around her. And she was listening. Then, all of a sudden, the lady saw a shoe. Then she saw some trousers and a shirt. Then a pink hand. And then the lady saw a nose with a big lump on it. She laughed and laughed because now she knew she had found what she was looking for.

"Billy boy," she called. "I've been hunting for you, everywhere. What has happened to your poor nose?"

Billy jumped up. "Mother," he shouted, "a mosquito bit me on the nose."

"Well, come along home," said Mother, "and we'll fix that funny lump."

As Billy and his mother started home for supper, Billy said, "I wonder how that mosquito could find me. I'm sure no other animal knew I was here in the grass." But, all unseen, the little mouse wiggled her whiskers and sniffed as two pairs of shoes walked past her. And, all unseen, the rabbit felt the earth tremble as the feet thumped, thumped away. And, all unseen, the squirrel heard Billy's voice. And high in the sky the great bird found out what was inside the shirt and trousers he had seen below him. And the mosquito thought, "Now I know it was Billy's nose that tasted so good!"

So all the animals found out what lay in the grass. They all found out that the shoe, the trousers and coat, the hand and the nose, really belonged to a little boy named Billy. And his mother knew this all the time! Did you?

The Lamby Sitter

BY LEE KINGMAN

Martha stood in her front yard, wondering what to do. It was cold outdoors, but she was so lonely playing by herself at home.

She looked across the hedge into the next yard, and then she ran as fast as she could to the house-next-door. Now she knew just what she wanted.

It wasn't one of Mrs. Snow's spicy, juicy apple pies, though they made the kitchen smell like an orchard in autumn.

What Martha wanted was in a corner of the kitchen. It was in a pen. It banged and rattled the bars and threw things. It shrieked and giggled. It kicked and cuddled. It was Mrs. Snow's baby, Sally.

Martha scooched down and handed the baby a toy duck, a monkey without a tail, and a chewed fish.

Sally chuckled and threw them out of the pen.

"I think she wants to come out," said Martha. "I could take her over to my playroom, or I could wheel her in her carriage."

"You just play with her right there, Martha," Mrs. Snow said.

"It's cold out."

"I could hold her and rock her and change her clothes," said Martha. "Or I could feed her! Mrs. Snow, let me take care of Sally! Please let me be a baby sitter."

"Oh, gracious goodness, Martha," said Mrs. Snow. "I do need one tomorrow, but I guess I'll have to take Sally with us. You'd be a fine baby sitter, if you were only a year or two older."

Martha pulled her eyebrows into a tight, fierce scowl, she tried so hard to look grown-up. Never in all her nine long years had she wanted anything so much as to be a baby sitter.

Sally shook the pen and shrieked, but Martha was so disappointed, she didn't feel like playing. She went outdoors.

"I'm sorry, Martha," Mrs. Snow called. "But you could and play with Sally whenever you like."

"Sally is too little to *play* with," Martha said to herself, she's just right to take care of. If only I could practice sitting, then Mrs. Snow would see I'm old enough."

But who was there to practice on?

Her dolls didn't wiggle when she dressed them.

There weren't any other children nearby, because the Snows' farm and the house where she lived with her Aunt and Uncle were all by themselves in the country.

Martha felt very lonely and much too little, just when she needed to be big.

"Martha!" Mr. Snow called. "Come see a surprise I found this morning."

She ran to the shelter where the big woolly sheep lived. There were two new wobbly little lambs.

"Twins!" said Mr. Snow proudly. "But I'm worried because their mother sometimes won't take care of two babies. And I have to go away tomorrow. Well, if the weather stays nice and warm and springlike, they'll get along."

He held the lambs for Martha to pat. Then she wandered home, still longing to be a baby sitter.

Early the next morning, Martha watched Mr. and Mrs. Snow and Sally start off in their truck. After lunch, Martha's Aunt said, "Why don't you play outdoors?"

So Martha walked around the yard, kicking dead leaves. But before she knew it, the sky clouded over, and something tickled her nose. A snowflake! The air shivered with snow!

Suddenly, she remembered the new lambs, and ran to the shelter. There were the big sheep. There was one of the twins! But where was the other?

Martha climbed the fence to see. In a corner, lying down, was a limp baby lamb!

Martha's heart thumped. Bravely, she opened the gate and slipped inside. Two big sheep pushed close and glared at her. She was very frightened, but she walked to the quiet lamb.

"He is cold and hungry and tired," Martha said, "and he needs someone to take care of him."

The sheep stamped restlessly in the swirling snow. Carefully, she lifted the lamb, and tucking him under her coat, carried him home.

Martha wanted the lamb all to herself, so she tiptoed into her playroom and shut the door.

She put a blanket in her doll's cradle. Then she slipped a doll's sweater over his floppy head and pushed his front feet through the sleeves. He wiggled a little! Not as much as a baby would wiggle—but so much more than a doll!

Carefully, she covered him up in the cradle. Then she filled her doll's hot water bottle and laid it beside him.

For a long time, Martha rocked the cradle and sang songs.

Suddenly, the lamb woke and spoke to her. "Baaa-aaa!" he said in a shrill, high little voice, just like a hungry baby!

"Oh, please don't cry!" begged Martha, "or Auntie will tell me to take you outside. Be a good baby, and go back to sleep!"

But the lamb cried harder than ever, "Baaaa-aa!"

Martha ran for some milk. While it warmed on her doll's

small stove, she rocked the cradle and sang very loud. The
lamb cried, "Baa-baa-baa!" in very good time to the music.

She poured the milk into a doll's bottle, but the lamb didn't
know how to drink it. He just cried louder than ever, "Baa-baa-
baa!"

Martha didn't know what to do, but she spilled some drops on
his nose. He licked them off, and began licking for more. So she
tried feeding him the bottle again, and soon he was sucking like
a noisy little engine. Before they knew it, the milk was all gone.

"Now that you have had a good nap and are all warm and
fed, you can get up and play." Martha held him, and although
he was now as full of wiggles as a brook, she put her doll's overalls on his hind feet. Then she put him down, and he stood still
and stiff in surprise, like a stuffed toy.

"Baa-aa!" he said to the plush elephant and the teddy bear.

"Let me put a bonnet on you, Lamby," said Martha.

But the lamb bounced away. His hoofs clacked over the floor!

"Hold still!" she cried, reaching for him. But she tripped and
fell. It sounded as if the sky were crashing in her bedroom. She
bumped her head and her knee hurt, but she didn't cry because
she didn't want Auntie to hear.

It was the lamb who cried at the top of his voice—"BAA-
BAA-BAA!"

Martha's Aunt opened the door. "Martha! What are you doing?"

"I'm taking care of Mr. Snow's lamb," said Martha. "Please let him stay. He's so little!"

"He may be little, but you are too big to bring animals in and wreck the house. Take it out at once."

Big tears choked Martha's throat, but she caught the lamb by his overalls, wrapped him up and carried him out.

She was too big to take care of animals and too little to take care of babies! She just wasn't anything at all! It was a horrid, empty feeling.

She saw the Snows had come home, so she knocked at the door. Mr. Snow came, and Martha handed him the bundle of lamb.

"So that's what happened to the poor little mite!" Mr. Snow laughed. "Come in, Martha, and tell us about it."

"I found the lamb all limp and cold and hungry," Martha said. "So I took him home and put him to bed with a hot water bottle, and then I fed him."

"You certainly did the right thing," said Mr. Snow. "I'm sure you saved his life."

Mrs. Snow was fixing a bottle for Sally, but she stopped to watch Mr. Snow unwrap the lamb. Martha was afraid they would laugh at the pink sweater and blue overalls, but they didn't. Mr. Snow just put the lamb in the play pen and lifted Sally out.

"Here, Martha—hold this," he said, and handed Sally to her.

"Would you like to feed her, Martha?" Mrs. Snow handed her Sally's bottle. "You'd better practice, because you might take care of Sally afternoons now and then."

"You mean I could be a baby sitter?" Martha cried.

"Why not!" said Mr. Snow. "You're the best lamby sitter we've ever had!"

Meow!

BY EVA GRANT

Siamese Cat! Siamese Cat!
 Royally crouched
 On your silken mat;

With your slanted eyes
Of sapphire blue,
And your slinky coat
Of tawny hue;

You are a beauty,
 Siamese Cat,
 But I wonder,
 Could you

C
a
t
 c
 h
 a
 r
 a
 t
 ?

What Would You Do If . . .

BY LEONORE KLEIN

What would you do IF you saw a rhinoceros coming down the street?

"If I saw a rhinoceros coming down the street," said Mike, the boy, "I'd tickle his ear, and he'd giggle and giggle and roll over and over and wag his tail."

"If *I* saw a rhinoceros coming down the street," said Dan, the man, "I'd step to the side, and he'd snort and cavort right into a tree with his sharp front horn. I'd be like a bullfighter and he'd be like a bull."

"I'd run away," said Susan, Mike's sister, "as fast as I could, and hide."

What would *you* do?

What would you do IF it snowed in summer?

"I'd write in the snow with my feet," said Mike. "I'd write with my footprints on somebody's lawn. 'Mr. Wimple is a pimple.' I think I'd write it on Mr. Wimple's lawn."

"Why?" asked Susan.

"Because he keeps our ball," said Mike.

"What would *you* do, Sue, if it snowed in summer?"

"I'd shiver," said Susan.

"I wouldn't shiver," said Dan, the man. "I'd turn on the oil burner and put on a jacket and get into bed under some blankets and read a book."

"I'd do something else," said Mike, the boy. "I'd build an igloo and spear a polar bear and make a rug for the igloo floor."

"What's an igloo?" asked Susan.

"An Eskimo house," said Mike.

How about you?

What would *you* do—if it snowed in summer?

What would you do IF your mother stopped smiling?

"If my mother stopped smiling," said Dan, the man, "I'd ask her to make me my favorite meal, corned beef and cabbage."

"Do *you* have a mother?" asked Susan and Mike.

"Of course I do," said Dan, the man. "And after I'd eaten and asked for some more, I'd say, 'What a good cook you are!' to my mother."

"What would you do, Susan and Mike, if *your* mother stopped smiling?"

"We'd climb in her lap," said Susan and Mike, "and hug her and kiss her. That's what we would do. Then she'd smile again."

IF someone just suddenly came up to you and said, "Here!" and gave you a bucket full up to the top with nothing but ice cream, what would you do then?

"You don't have to ask what I would do," said Mike, the boy.

"No," said Susan, "but can you eat *two* buckets full? I'll let you have mine. I like jelly beans better than ice cream."

"I'd put mine in the freezer," said Dan, the man, "so that I'd have some tomorrow and the day after tomorrow and the day after that."

What would *you* do?

What would you do IF someone gave you 100 pillows?

"Oh, boy!" said Mike. "I'd cut them open with my pocket-knife, and throw them in the air. And the millions and billions and trillions of feathers would make a blizzard and hide the sun. And boys would make feather balls and throw them. And girls would make feather men. And babies would wear galoshes!"

"I'd take just one pillow." said Susan, "just one. And I'd give it to my doll for a feather bed."

"I'd sneeze," said Dan. "Feathers make me sneeze."

Some people would pile all the pillows into one great pile and climb to the top—and bounce!

What would *you* do?

What would you do IF three bad guys . . . brought a great bunch of cowboys on palomino horses shooting and tooting and plundering and thundering right into town where the girls and their mothers were buying dresses in department stores?

"All bad guys?" asked Mike.

All bad guys. Of course.

"Then," said Mike, "I'd shoot from the hip with both my guns, fast on the draw as buttery lightning:

Bang-a-Bang-Bang!

Bang-a-Bang-Bang!

"And bunches would die. And bunches would run."

"Run for cover?" asked Susan.

"For cover," said Mike.

"All *I* would do," said Dan, the man, "is to tell them all in a deep, loud voice, 'There are women and children here. Remember?'"

"And," asked Mike and Susan, holding their breaths, "what would happen then?"

"The bunch of cowboys would lower their guns and turn their horses and head out of town very slowly, and gently, and quietly."

"Why?" asked Susan and Mike.

"Because cowboys are good to women and children," said Dan, the man. "Even the bad guys."

"Oh," said Susan. "Well, then, I'd just grab Mother's hand and squeeze it tight, and we'd go upstairs on the escalator and buy me a dress and a stiff petticoat."

"I might do something else," said Mike, the boy. "I might look for a pony—a palomino pony that had lost its cowboy—and take it home and give it some sugar."

"Gee, how I'd like a palomino pony!"

If you were catching beetles in a large, glass jar, and a small, spotted beetle suddenly said,

"Put me back in the grass. Put me back, kind sir, and I'll grant you a wish, any wish in the world."

What would you wish for?

"I'd wish," said Dan, the man, "for something I could do that would make me proud. Like making a boat with a saw and some wood and a hammer and nails—a strong, little boat I could use for fishing. I'd fish for swordfish or maybe for sharks. Or, better than that," said Dan, the man, "I'd wish to play music —music that would make you want to dance."

"I'd wish for a puppy," said Mike, the boy, "and a B-B gun, and a football helmet, and a hundred hot dogs, and a catcher's mitt, and a two-wheeler bike, and some small white mice, and, of course, the pony. That's all I want," said Mike, the boy, in one big breath.

"All I'd wish for," said Susan, "is a baby brother or a baby sister. Just the size of my doll, but real!"

What would *you* wish for?

A Nickel for a Pickle

BY ROSALIE LOWELL

What fun to earn a nickel! Johnny Jackson held it in the palm of his hand and admired the big fat buffalo on one side. He turned it over and smiled at the strong face of the Indian. "Needs to be shinier," he thought, even though Mrs. Carroll had carefully picked out the shiniest one she had after Johnny had walked her dog around the block for her three times.

"Yop, needs to be shinier," Johnny said to himself. So first he spit on it and then he rubbed it hard and fast on the back of his pants.

There, that was better, except for that one deep scratch on the buffalo's head he just couldn't dig out. Now that it was shinier, the buffalo seemed to look even larger and the Indian seemed to be smiling back at him.

"Shame to spend such a nice shiny nickel," he said. But that's just what he planned to do. He could get a pickle for a nickel and that's what he wanted. Johnny loved pickles. Just thinking of one made his mouth water. His mouth watered even more when he thought of that great big jar of pickles the Pickle Shop always had on its counter. A great big jar full of pickles with a big card on top that read "A Nickel for a Pickle."

He held the nickel tight in his hand, then put it in his pocket. "Safer there," he thought as he dashed full speed ahead to the Pickle Shop. He hoped they would be good and sour, the way he liked his pickles. Yum, yum, he could feel the pickle juice trickling down his mouth, sliding down his chin. And before he knew it, he was in the Pickle Shop.

Johnny dug down into his pocket for his nickel, but his fingers didn't feel it. He dug deeper. No nickel. "Oh no," he thought, "I just had it." And he dug down some more. He even yanked the pocket inside out, but all he could see was a hole at the end, the size of a nickel. "Oh," he said, "I lost my big shiny nickel. Oh, it can't be," he cried. And Mr. Kraus, who stood behind the counter, said, "No nickel, no pickle."

Meanwhile, Johnny Jackson's nickel was lying on the pavement outside the Pickle Shop looking brighter than ever with the sun shining on it. And who should come along but Ellen, carrying her pretty little bag. "What a surprise!" she said, stooping down to pick up the nickel. "I know just what I'll get —some new jacks." And off she skipped around the block. But just as she was thinking of her new jacks, snap went one of her shoestrings! "Oh, not again!" she said. But she knew if she didn't stop to fix it, her shoestring would get looser and looser and by and by her shoe would slip off. "I'll lean against that car," she said. "It'll be easier to fix," and she carefully put her pretty little bag on the car's hood, bent over, and tied a fat knot in her shoestring. "There, that'll do," she thought, "until Mommy gets me a brand-new pair." And Ellen went right on skipping toward the store to buy her new jacks.

Meanwhile, Johnny Jackson's nickel was in Ellen's bag where she had left it on the hood of the car. And who should come along and spot it but Peter holding a loaf of bread. "Oh," he said, "a girl's bag. What will I do with it anyway? Guess I can give it to my sister." But he was hoping awfully hard that there was something in it for *him.* Sure enough, when he opened the bag, there at the bottom, was the nickel.

"Oh great!" he shouted, "a nickel, just what I need! Now I can get a new string for my top." And off he ran home with the loaf of bread his mother was waiting for. But just as Peter got there, he remembered his favorite cowboy program was on and he hated to miss it. He dropped the bread for his mother, he dropped the bag for his sister. He hurried so that he dropped the nickel too. But no one heard the nickel drop, because Peter's mother was using the vacuum cleaner and so up the vacuum cleaner went Johnny Jackson's nickel.

But just as Peter's mother was going to empty the vacuum bag, the bell rang and there was her neighbor at the door saying, "Oh dear, I hate to be a nuisance, but may I borrow your vacuum cleaner for just a little while? Ours went out of order and, oh dear, we have guests visiting us any minute now."

"Of course," Peter's mother said. "Just let me clean it out first." But her neighbor said, "Don't bother, I'm really in such a hurry. I'll take it just the way it is." And off she rushed with the vacuum to tidy up her house.

Meanwhile, Johnny Jackson's nickel was lying in the vacuum in the middle of a lot of dirt. But the nickel didn't stay there very long, because in no time at all, Mrs. Jackson had whisked through her house and was emptying the vacuum bag, so she could return it nice and clean. She spread a newspaper on the floor to dump all the dirt on. Good gracious, all the stuff and things that came out of that vacuum! Scraps of paper, hairpins, chunks of dirt, marbles and bobby pins, nails and screws, orange peel, peanut shells. Even a wad of bubble gum came tumbling out of that vacuum and, of course, Johnny Jackson's nickel, black as black can be.

And who should come into the room at that very moment but Johnny Jackson himself, looking sad.

"Why, what's wrong, sweetie?" Mrs. Jackson asked.

"Lost the nickel I earned," Johnny said, looking even sadder.

"Oh dear, what a shame! But don't worry about it," Mrs. Jackson said, "maybe you'll find it."

"Nope, don't think I will," Johnny answered, "I have a hole in my pocket."

"I'll sew it later," his mother said. "Look, honey. See what

came out of the vacuum cleaner. It almost looks like a nickel. Do you suppose it is? It's covered with so much dirt, I'm not at all sure."

"Let's see," Johnny said, taking it from her hand. And he took the nickel and first he spit on it and then he rubbed it hard and fast on the back of his pants until it became shinier and shinier.

"It sure is! How did a nickel get in there anyway? Look at it, Mom! Just see how brave the Indian looks now." And he turned the nickel over and said, "And just look at that big fat buffalo, gosh, isn't he . . ." But before he even finished his sentence, he let out a great big whoop! "Gol-*ly* he yelled. "It's *my* nickel, it's *my* nickel!"

"*Your* nickel?" his mother asked. "Why I borrowed this vacuum cleaner from Peter's mother."

"Sure as shootin', it's *my* nickel, it sure is!" Johnny Jackson yelled. "Look at the buffalo, Mom. Look real close now and you'll see a little scratch right on his head. "See it, see it? That's the nickel I earned this morning. I noticed the scratch on the buffalo's head the minute I shined it up. Yippee! I lost that nickel, but now it came back to me!"

"Goodness gracious," his mother said, looking hard at the scratch on the buffalo's head. "What a surprise to get your nickel back. It's just wonderful! It certainly *is* the nickel you lost. I can see that scratch very clearly. Just imagine!"

"I can hardly believe it, Mommy," Johnny said. "It's like magic!"

"What are you going to do with it, Johnny?" she asked.

"I think I'll keep it," Johnny said, "It's such a lucky nickel."

And then he thought of the Pickle Shop. Yum, yum. He could feel the pickle juice trickling down his mouth, sliding down his chin. He could buy a pickle for that nickel or he could save it for good luck. He knew just what he was going to do with that nickel. Do you?

Easter Treat

BY ROGER DUVOISIN

It was springtime; nearly Easter.

Santa Claus stood at the window of his warm igloo at the North Pole and beheld the snow-covered plain which spread far out to meet the grey sky.

"My dear," said Santa to Mrs. Santa, "sometimes I grow tired of icy winds and snowflakes. I want to take a vacation from my toymaking. I want to go and see the spring flowers."

"But Santa," said Mrs. Santa, "you cannot show yourself when it isn't Christmas! What will people think?"

"Oh, I know," sang Santa.

> *My red coat and my white beard,*
> *Christmas trees and Poinsettias,*
> *Plum puddings and gay wrappings,*

only come in wintertime when the snow is on the ground; when the trees are bare and black; when the birds forget to sing. Well, this spring I want to see the daffodils and the tulips bloom; hear the birds sing among the lilac buds; walk along streets bright with spring sun."

"I think you are foolish," scolded Mrs. Santa. "How funny you will look with your red coat when people have long forgotten about Christmas. You may be arrested."

"Ah," smiled Santa, "but I will go IN-COG-NI-TO which means no one will know who I am. I will dress like a tourist and leave my red suit here in the closet."

Santa picked the mail-order catalog from a shelf and wrote an order for a complete new outfit for his trip.

When the package came, he was as happy as a child at Christmas.

He unwrapped an elegant felt hat, a well-creased pair of slacks with yellow suspenders, a beautiful plaid tweed coat, a white shirt, a bow tie with polka dots, so pretty that Santa thought it was a shame that his beard covered it, a smart pair of shiny shoes, and an umbrella for the spring rains. "You look very handsome!" cried Mrs. Santa with pride.

The next day Santa harnessed his reindeer and flew to the nearest airport. He could not ride his sleigh all the way to the warmer country, because there was no more snow to land on.

Then he boarded a plane which flew him to the big city.

How different the city looked at Eastertime!

"It's a new city," thought Santa. "Fresh and gay and filled with flowers."

He sat in the park in the warm sun and watched the robins hop on the lawn and the sparrows gather twigs for their nests.

He strolled through the streets where flower carts replaced the Christmas tree stands he had seen on his last trip; where the store windows were decorated with tulips, daffodils, and forsythia, with big sugar Easter eggs, with white rabbits and cotton chicks.

He admired the pretty women who had put away their fur coats and wore light straw hats and bright dresses. And he nodded at the men who walked lightly with smiles on their faces.

Santa wanted to look like Easter, too. So he bought a fresh daffodil to stick in his lapel. And he walked along the street feeling warm and happy.

He even whistled "Jingle Bells!" But he stopped short because people began to stare at him. "Jingle Bells" at Eastertime!

"Oh, well," thought Santa, "I am really incognito. No one will know me."

When he turned the corner, Santa found himself in a street full of children playing jump rope and marbles.

As he stood there, watching, a small girl came to him dancing and singing,

> *Oh, see the little old man.*
> *He snatched Santa's white beard;*
> *he stole Santa's red nose;*
> *and wears his gay twinkle.*

Santa was surprised. He wanted to travel incognito, but he
did not want to be taken for a thief.

"You are quite wrong, my child," he said. "I stole nothing
from Santa Claus."

But more children came and formed a ring around Santa.
They danced and sang,

> *Yes you did,*
> *yes you did.*
> *His white beard,*
> *his red nose,*
> *his gay twinkle,*
> *you stole from dear Santa.*

Santa was so astonished now that he even forgot he didn't
want anyone to know who he was.

> *But, my children," he cried,*
> *this is* MY *white beard,*
> *this is* MY *red nose*
> *this is* MY *gay twinkle.*
> I AM SANTA CLAUS!

The children only laughed.

> *No, you aren't,*
> *no, you aren't.*
> *Santa has big black boots.*
> *Santa has a red coat.*
> *Santa has a red cap.*
> *Santa never comes when Christmas has gone.*

They would not believe Santa was Santa.

Many people who were passing stopped to watch. Soon there was a crowd listening to this little old man who cried,

"I AM SANTA CLAUS."

Now, a policeman made his way through the crowd and asked, "What's the matter here?"

"There is a little old man," cried the children, "who says he is Santa Claus."

"Yes, Officer," said Santa, "I *am* Santa Claus."

"Is that so?" said the policeman. "Santa Claus, hey? Well, I think you had better come with me."

And he put his hand on Santa's shoulder and led him to police headquarters, followed by all the children.

"This little old man," said the policeman to the captain behind the desk, "pretends he is Santa Claus and is disturbing the peace in our street."

"That's bad," said the captain, with an especially deep policeman's voice. "We cannot allow this sort of thing in our town."

"But I AM SANTA CLAUS," shouted Santa Claus.

"No one can shout here but me," said the captain severely.

"Look, Captain Hooligan," began Santa, "I . . ."

"How do you know my name?" interrupted the captain.

"Santa knows everything," said Santa, "EVERYTHING. I can tell you what I dropped into your chimney last Christmas. There were blue pajamas for you, a wrist watch for your wife, Alice, and an electric train for your boy, Bobby. Do you believe I am Santa *now?*"

"Plum puddings and Easter eggs!" exclaimed the captain in astonishment. "That *is* what Santa left for us last Christmas."

"I also know, Captain," said Santa with a happy twinkle, "that you exchanged your blue pajamas for a pair with flowers on them."

"My wife liked the ones with flowers best," said the Captain.

"Then you should have flowers," said Santa. "Now I will show you again that Santa knows and remembers everything."

And he turned to the children who were crowded near the door and called them in, one by one, by their first names.

"This is Mary. I brought her a Dutch doll with a blue dress on Christmas day. Your doll has lost her wooden shoes, Mary. Look under the kitchen stove where the kitten was playing with them.

"This is William, who paints such beautiful pictures with the paintbox I gave him. Do not paint on the wallpaper, William.

"This is Ann. I left a stuffed polar bear for her, just like the real ones I see around my igloo.

"This is Dolly, who found a silver necklace in her sock.

"And Tommy, who got a baseball outfit.

"And Ted, and Nora, and Billy, and Jimmy . . ."

But no one was listening to Santa any more. All the children and the passers-by crowded around him and hugged him and kissed him until his elegant felt hat was crushed flat on top of his head, and his fresh daffodil hung limp from his lapel.

"Dear old Santa . . . dear old Santa . . ." the captain and the policeman repeated tenderly over and over again.

After the hugging and kissing, they all went out for a stroll through the town to show Santa more of the gay Easter trimmings. And they took him through the stores where they bought piles of presents for him and for Mrs. Santa.

It was amidst a big cheering crowd that Santa finally left by plane for the airport far north where his sleigh was waiting. He was so happy, he was all smiles and twinkles.

Santa's sleigh had always left the North Pole full of gifts for others. But this time it was different. It was *returning* home filled with presents for Santa and Mrs. Santa. There were sugar Easter eggs, chocolate Easter eggs, plain eggs and decorated eggs, big eggs with small eggs inside, sugar bunnies and stuffed bunnies, a live white bunny with a yellow ribbon, cotton chicks and live chicks, bunches and bunches of daffodils, tulips, narcissus, and a beautiful Easter dress and a pretty flowered hat for Mrs. Santa.

Santa and Mrs. Santa had a very cheerful Easter indeed. Afterwards, when Santa went back to his toymaking, he knew that next Christmas he would load his sleigh with the most beautiful toys he had ever made.

Stripes and Spots

BY DAHLOV IPCAR

Once there was a tiger, a little striped tiger. He was striped with stripes, beautiful gold tiger stripes, from the tip of his nose to the tip of his tail. He was just a baby tiger and he lived in a cave in the jungle with his mother and his father and his brother and his sister. And they were all of them striped with stripes as stripey as they could be.

One warm day the little tiger woke up from his afternoon nap and he stretched his claws and he stretched his jaws and he stretched himself. Then he said to himself, "I'm hungry, I'm very hungry. I'm going out in the jungle and catch myself something to eat." So he went out into the big green jungle.

He padded softly along under the leafy trees. It was hot in the jungle, in the big green jungle. It was dark under the trees, tangled and green and damp. The little tiger walked boldly through the jungle waving his striped tail looking for something to catch.

In another cave in the jungle there lived a little spotted leopard. He was just a baby leopard, but he was spotted and dotted from head to toe with beautiful round black spots. He lived with *his* mother and *his* father and *his* brother and sister, and they were all of them spotted and dotted as spotty as they could be.

The little leopard woke up too that warm afternoon, and he stretched and he yawned and he said to himself, "I'm hungry, I'm very hungry. I wish I had something nice to eat." So out he went into the big wild jungle.

It was hot and damp and green and tangled. As the little leopard prowled along on his soft feet he smelled all the wonderful jungle smells. He was very, very hungry and he wanted very much to catch something to eat.

And there in the jungle the little striped tiger met the little spotted leopard. First they sniffed noses and rubbed whiskers to say hello. Then the little tiger said. "What are you doing here?"

And the little leopard said, "I'm hunting. I'm hunting for something to eat because I'm hungry."

"That's just what I'm doing too," said the little tiger. "Let's go hunting together."

"Fine," said the little leopard. "If we find something with stripes you can catch it, and if we find something with spots, I can catch it."

So they both rubbed whiskers again, just to show they agreed, and then they walked along together through the tangled green jungle, prowling softly through the sunlight and the shadow under the trees.

The little tiger found some striped bugs crawling up the grasses, and he ate one but it didn't taste very good.

The little leopard found some spotted bugs crawling on the ground. He ate three, but they didn't taste good at all.

The little tiger saw a striped chipmunk sitting on a log. He

almost caught the little chipmunk, but the chipmunk scurried down a hole, and though he waited and waited it wouldn't come out.

The little leopard found a round spotted turtle crawling along the ground. He pounced on it, but the turtle pulled his head and feet into his shell, and even though they waited and waited, it wouldn't come out.

The little tiger found some pretty striped leaves and flowers. He tried to eat them, but they didn't taste very good. They didn't taste much like tiger food.

The little leopard found some beautiful spotted flowers and leaves, and he tried to eat them too, but they didn't taste very good to him. They didn't taste much like leopard food.

Then they saw some striped butterflies flying through the sunlight. The little tiger tried to catch them, but they flew away, high up over his head, high up in the green tree tops.

And high up where the butterflies flew were the little monkeys and the big monkeys swinging by their long arms, swing-ing by their long tails, swinging and holding on with their feet, with the little monkeys riding on their mothers' backs. All the monkeys chattered, *chee, chee, chee,* and yelled and laughed and screeched and threw sticks at the little tiger and the little leop-ard. So they crept away as quietly as they could on their soft padded paws.

They came at last to a wide slow river winding through the trees, and they saw some little spotted birds hopping about on the shore near the water's edge. The little leopard tried to catch them, but they flew up and away across the wide river. He stood and watched them go.

Then the little leopard and the little tiger padded softly along beside the river, looking for something to catch. Some-thing not too little and not too fast, something that couldn't fly or climb to the tree tops, something with stripey stripes or spotty spots, something that would taste good to a little striped tiger or a little spotted leopard.

As they followed the river's edge they saw the crocodiles floating in the water like big sunken logs. They hid in the tall grass and watched them; and while they watched, a herd of slim spotted deer came slowly through the trees to drink at the river's banks.

The little leopard crept closer, but a big crocodile opened his mouth, showing rows and rows of white teeth, and roared and lashed his tail and chased the little leopard and the little tiger back up the bank.

And just then they heard another roar right behind them!

They saw something big moving through the bushes. It seemed to have stripes and it seemed to have spots too.

They crouched down and they scrunched up all trembly with fright as they heard a voice say, "Just what we're looking for, a little striped tiger and a little spotted leopard."

It was their mothers!

The little tiger and the little leopard were both very glad to
see their mothers, because they knew they would have something for them to eat, and they were both very, very hungry.

They all walked happily back home together, and when they
got home they had supper.

They had milk for supper. It wasn't striped, and it wasn't
spotted. It was white, as milk always is, and it tasted very, very
good to both of them.

Then, when he was full, the little tiger said to himself,
"Some things have stripes, and some things have spots and
some things are plain, but if they are good to eat, I don't care."

Then he curled up with his brother and his sister and his
mother, all happy and purring and sleepy.

The little leopard curled up too with *his* mother and *his*
sister and brother, all full and sleepy and purring. Soon they
were all sound asleep, safe and warm in their caves, while outside the rain fell softly in the dark, green jungle night.

Pancho

BY BERTA AND ELMER HADER

Don Fernando, the richest man in the village, was angry!

A wild bull with a crooked tail coaxed the best cattle in his herd to run away.

So Don Fernando offered a purse filled with gold to anyone who caught the bull with the crooked tail.

Cowboys from nearby ranches came to win the prize. First Alfonso rode out on the range. He was sure he would win the purse filled with gold.

But the wild bull ran away with Alfonso's broken lasso trailing from his horns.

Alfonso went home.

"I'll win the prize," shouted Carlos as he galloped away in a cloud of dust.

Carlos lost his hat as well as his lasso, but he did *not* win the prize.

Then Jose, Juan, and Paco tried and failed. No one could catch the bull.

Don Fernando grew angrier and angrier. He offered a silver-trimmed saddle and the biggest hat in all Mexico as well as the purse to anyone who caught the wild bull.

He put the prizes in the window of his store for everyone to see.

All the best riders on the finest horses in the whole state came to try to win the prize.

Every day these cowboys rode past the adobe hut where Pedro, the potter, lived with his wife and young son Pancho. The little family made pots, plates, and bowls to sell in the village. Every morning Pancho led his little burro to the market place.

Pancho often stopped to look at the big hat and the saddle trimmed with silver in the window of Don Fernando's store. No one wanted to win the reward more than Pancho. But he was only a little boy and he had no swift horse nor fine lasso with which to capture the wild bull.

Early one morning Pancho loaded his burro with all the pots his father had made and all the gay colored plates his mother had painted and set out for the market place. As he walked along he thought how fine it would be to ride in a saddle trimmed with silver, wearing the biggest hat in all Mexico, and how happy he could make his father and mother with the purse filled with gold.

"Heee-Haw!" The burro stopped at the turn in the road and so did Pancho.

Right in the middle of the road stood the *wild bull* with the crooked tail!

The cowboys' broken lassos trailed from his horns and he was angry.

Pancho turned about and the burro turned, too. They ran as fast as they could.

Whipped by the lassos, the bull ran after Pancho and the burro.

He knocked the pack from the burro's back! ! Pots, plates, and bowls rolled in all directions. The bull kept running and Pancho felt his hot breath just as he scrambled to safety in a big oak that grew beside the road. The bull stamped on Pancho's hat and tossed his head. He snorted and bellowed. He was a very mad bull.

"*Vamos,*" shouted Pancho. But the bull would not go away. Pancho was a prisoner in the tree!

He wondered what to do. He looked at the lassos trailing from the bull's horns and thought hard.

Then he broke a hooked branch from the tree. Quickly he fished up the nearest lasso and fastened it firmly around the trunk of the tree. The bull pawed the ground angrily and moved closer.

Pancho fished up the other lasso and tied it firmly, too. Then he jumped to the ground and ran.

The bull charged after Pancho, but the lassos soon stopped him.

He bellowed and stamped his hoofs in a rage, but he could not get away. He was tied fast to the tree. The wild bull with the crooked tail was now a prisoner.

Pancho caught his burro and hurried home to tell what had happened.

"*MAMACITA, PAPACITO!*" shouted Pancho, "I've caught the *wild bull!*"

His father and mother hurried down the road to see for themselves.

Just then Don Fernando and his cowboys came back from the cattle range. They stared at the bull tied to the tree and they looked in amazement at Pancho and his burro. The news spread fast.

The mayor hurried to the oak tree followed by most of the villagers. It was true!

Pancho, the potter's son, had captured the wild bull with the crooked tail. The mayor proclaimed a holiday in honor of the occasion.

The next day Pancho wore the biggest hat in all Mexico and sat in a saddle trimmed with silver as he led the procession through the village streets and around the market place. Then Don Fernando gave him the purse filled with gold.

"Viva, viva!" shouted the villagers. Pancho was happy.

With the gold in the purse, Pancho bought his father a motor car to ride in, and he bought a new dress and a bright red shawl for his mother. They were all very happy.

Now that his cattle were safe Don Fernando was happy too.

Everyone was happy except the wild bull with the crooked tail. He had to stay in a pen with a brass ring in the end of his nose.

How Gerald McGrew Caught the Filla-Ma-Zokk

BY DR. SEUSS

On the farthest-up rock, in the Mountains of Mokk,
Lives a beast called the Ram-Tazzled Filla-ma-Zokk.
And of all of the beasts I've brought back to my zoo.
The catching of him was the hardest to do.

That beast is so big that you never could hope
To drag him back home to your zoo on a rope.
Too smart to be caged and too tough to be fought,
There's only one way he can ever be caught:
If you climb up the mountains and get on his track
And play the right music, he'll follow you back!

But the music he'll come for can only be played
On a musical instrument which, I'm afraid,
Costs three thousand dollars and ninety-eight cents.
It's called the o'Grunth. The o'Grunth is immense,
and its scale doesn't have any notes that you know
Like re and like mi and like sol, la, ti, do.
For, instead of a fa,
It has sort of a bah
And, instead of a la, it has sort of a gah
And, instead of a ti, the o'Grunth has a pooh!
And, instead of a mi, it has sort of a you!
And, to play that o'Grunth
Took me more than a month
Of practicing, practicing!
Wasn't much fun-th.
And, boy! Was it heavy! Weighed almost a ton-th.
It's the kind of a thing that I'll only do one-th.

Mr. Scrunch

THE STORY OF AN INVENTOR AND HIS ANIMAL FRIENDS
BY HELEN AND ALF EVERS

Mr. Jasper Scrunch was a very famous inventor. Kindness shone from his pink face, which was set off by white hair and whiskers.

But Mr. Scrunch was clever as well as kind. So he had spent his life inventing thousands of machines to help people and to make them happier. His machines made it easier for people to work, easier for them to play, and even easier for them to do nothing at all.

Mr. Scrunch invented a dresser and undresser. This clever machine, which looked like a comfortable chair, could take off or put on the clothes of anyone sitting in it, in a few seconds. It could also sew on missing buttons, mend tears, and remove spots and stains while it dressed or undressed.

This machine was sold all over the world, except in those uncivilized places, such as the South Sea Islands, where people don't wear enough clothes to make it worth while.

Mr. Scrunch was also the inventor of a sled which could coast uphill faster than it could downhill.

A few more of Mr. Scrunch's inventions were a self-making bed, a rocking chair which rocked itself, and for very *lazy* people, a game-playing machine, which played baseball, tennis, cards, or croquet for them.

These inventions made Mr. Scrunch rich.

But Mr. Scrunch worked so very, very hard at inventing things to keep other people from working that he became very tired. His friends insisted that he take a vacation.

So the inventor bought a quiet little farm, on a quiet little road near a quiet little village, and went there to take a long rest. When Mr. Scrunch reached the farm, he hired two men to do the farm work. Then he sat down on the steps and did nothing for ten minutes.

As Mr. Scrunch sat on the steps, doing nothing, he saw four little pigs racing round and round the barn. One of the pigs was always last, because he had very short legs. Mr. Scrunch felt sorry for him.

So he coaxed the pig into the house with a bowl of milk and a banana. Then, while the pig was busy eating, Mr. Scrunch thought hard and invented something to help the short-legged pig run faster. The invention was remarkably simple. It was just four little stilts with straps to hold them in place.

First, kind Mr. Scrunch tested the stilts himself. It was so much fun that he hated to take them off.

Then he put the stilts on the pig. Away went the little pig, tumbling down at every step. Down went chairs and tables, lamps and pictures.

And down went Mr. Scrunch. The pig raced faster and faster

as he learned how to manage the stilts. At last he vanished through the open door.

Mr. Scrunch sat on the floor, a picture frame around his neck and a lamp cord around his legs.

"Dear me!" he murmured. "That worked altogether too well, but never mind, it has given me a *tremendous idea.*"

"All these years," said Mr. Scrunch unwinding the lamp cord, "I have been inventing things to help people, but I have never thought of making inventions to help animals do their work and enjoy their play. Someone must do it," he said solemnly, "and that someone will be me."

He removed the picture frame from his neck and began.

First, he invented prettier and more comfortable hats for the horses to wear in hot weather.

Then he invented an automatic fly swatter, to save the horses the trouble of swishing their tails all day in hot weather. As the swatter revolved, it produced a gentle breeze which kept the horses cool, even on the hottest day.

Mr. Scrunch hated to see the hens sleeping at night clinging to their hard roost. So he invented comfortable beds with soft pillows for them.

He invented little sails for the ducks to use on the pond, so that they would not have to work so hard at swimming.

And finally Mr. Scrunch invented a grazing machine for Belle, the old cow.

For a long time Mr. Scrunch had felt sorry for cows, because they had to work so hard grazing. It didn't seem right to him that cows should spend most of the day with their faces practically on the ground, tugging away at the grass and sometimes picking up insects, thorns, sand, or even stones, by mistake.

So Mr. Scrunch invented a machine, something like a lawn mower, with a fan in front and a basket on top, to be strapped to Belle. As Belle walked, the mower cut the grass, the fan blew everything but the grass away, and all Belle had to do was to eat from the basket right in front of her mouth.

But when the horses had their hats and automatic fly swatters they had so little to do, when they were in the pasture in the summer, that they couldn't stand it.

So they jumped over the fence into Mr. Scrunch's fine cornfield and ate and ate cornstalks until they became very sick.

Then the veterinary had to come and cure them with some bitter medicine.

When the hens tried their new beds they found them so comfortable that they couldn't get up in the morning and get to work laying eggs.

When the ducks were fitted with their sails a breeze came up, and they just whirled round and round the ponds like tops until they became dizzy.

And Belle, the cow, loved the old way of grazing and hated Mr. Scrunch's grazing machine so much that when she first tried it she became so angry that she raced across the fields, kicking her heels in the air, with Mr. Scrunch after her.

She crossed the road and raced right through the poppies and roses in Mrs. Green's garden, leaving a smooth path behind her and chopped-up flowers flying through the air.

On she went through Mr. Jenkins' vegetable patch, mowing down the neat rows of carrots and lettuce.

And on she raced across the lawn where Mrs. Anderson had spread her best cloths and napkins to bleach in the sun.

The chopped-up bits of white cloth swirled in the air around Belle like snowflakes in a blizzard.

At last, with a crash that could be heard for miles, Belle smashed the grazing machine against a stone wall. Then she felt much better.

Mr. Scrunch came up, puffing and panting. First he paid Mrs. Green, Mrs. Anderson, and Mr. Jenkins, who had arrived full of anger and threats, for the damage done by the grazing machine.

As he led Belle home, Mr. Scrunch patted her affectionately.

"Dear me," he murmured. "This is all too bad, but never mind, it has given me an idea for a tremendous invention to help animals."

For days Mr. Scrunch slaved away at his invention, hardly stopping to eat or sleep. It looked like an immense box, with a sort of coffee mill on top. When it was finished he put it in the barnyard and called all the animals together.

Mr. Scrunch took the stilts from the pig, the sails from the ducks, the beds from the henhouse, and the hats and automatic fly swatters from the horses. He put them all, one by one, in the top of the machine. Then he pressed a button.

There was a sighing, wheezing noise from inside the machine. A little puff of blue smoke popped out, hovered over the machine for a moment, and slowly sailed away.

This was all that was left of Mr. Scrunch's invention for animals.

"Hurrah," cried Mr. Scrunch, "for the last and best of my

inventions for animals—Scrunch's Univerasl Uninventor for Useless Inventions!"

Then Mr. Scrunch put one arm around Belle and the other on one of the horses. A chicken flew to the top of his head and a happy duck to his shoulder, while a pig rubbed his side against the inventor's legs.

"At last," said Mr. Scrunch in a voice made unsteady by emotion, "at last I have invented something that has helped all of you and made you happy. All my work has not been in vain."

And then kind Mr. Scrunch, with a smile on his face, went to the house, sat down on the steps, and did nothing at all for a long, long time.

Nino and His Fish

BY EDITH THATCHER HURD AND CLEMENT HURD

Little Nino sat thinking. He was thinking about his birthday that was coming in just a few days and Nino knew there would be no birthday party. That is, there would be no birthday party unless his father's luck changed.

Nino's father, Tony, was a fisherman. He fished for sardines from August to Christmas and for salmon from May to the Fourth of July. But this year there had been few sardines and they had gone away early while the salmon were late in coming and very hard to catch. And little Nino knew that if a fisherman doesn't catch fish, he doesn't have money for birthdays.

Nino sat thinking. He smelled the salt smell of the sea. He listened to the far away fog horn.

"Whoo-oo-oo."

It was a sad sound. "Whoo-oo-oo." It made little Nino sad too.

Then suddenly he jumped up. He ran quickly into the house to find his mother.

"I have an idea," he spoke quickly. "A wonderful idea. What if, what if my father would let me go fishing with him? What if I should go fishing and what if I should catch a fish of my own? A great big fish! Then I could invite all my friends and we would eat fish for my party."

Nino's mother looked at him gently and smiled.

"And you would not mind if you had no cake, little Nino?" she asked. "I cannot buy eggs and butter and all the good things that go into a real birthday cake."

Nino was quiet for a moment thinking about a birthday without any birthday cake. But then he laughed.

"Who cares about cake? Fish is fine for a birthday."

Nino could hardly wait for his father to come home that night so that he could ask him if he would let him go fishing with him the next day.

At first Tony said, "No. I have all I can do to tend to my own fishing let alone looking out for you, little Nino."

"But I will be no trouble," pleaded Nino. "I will just sit quietly. Perhaps I could even watch some of your lines for you."

"Well," Tony smiled at last. "You will really be good then? Not talk too much or ask too many questions?"

The next morning Nino was the first in the house to be awake. He must not keep his father waiting. The sun was barely up when the two set out for the Fisherman's Wharf. Nino carried his long fishing pole and Tony carried their lunch.

Nino loved the Fisherman's Wharf better than any place he knew. He loved the smell of fish everywhere; the smell of the new ropes and the paint smell and the salt smell of the sea.

Nino and Tony walked together past Anastasia's Fish Market with its rows of fish all spread out neatly on their bed of shaved ice. There was a big pink salmon; a red rock cod and the crimson crabs with their crooked claws sticking up in the air. There were the squids with their silver and black eyes; the big black eels and the purple, spiny sea urchins in boxes.

Almost at the end of the Fisherman's Wharf was Angelo's. Now Angelo's was a very fine restaurant. It was painted pink and blue on the outside. Nino and his friends had often peeked in through the big windows at night and seen the elegant waiters in their black coats with white napkins folded over their arms. They bustled about among the square tables covered with crisp white tablecloths. The silver knives and forks gleamed in the candlelight, and from the kitchen at the back of the restaurant there always came the smell of wonderful things to eat.

But Angelo's was not a place for the fishermen. No, only the tourists ate at Angelo's while the fishermen went to the little fish houses up and down the wharf where they sat on high stools and ate off narrow counters covered with red and white oilcloth.

This morning Angelo himself stood by his pink and blue door watching the fisherman go by. As soon as he saw Tony and Nino he waved.

"So," he called. "You are turned fisherman, Nino?"

Nino smiled and felt proud that Angelo should speak to him like this in front of everyone.

"Yes," he answered. "I am going fishing with my father to catch a big fish for my birthday. I shall ask all my friends to come."

"Ho-ho-ho!" laughed Angelo. "A fish for a birthday. Who would ever want fish for a birthday? That's no good. Why, my

little Nino, for a birthday you must have chicken and sausage
and ravioli and gnocchi and pizza and salami and then most
of all you must have a cake. You surely were going to have a
cake, little Nino?"

Nino did not know how to answer. He looked quickly to see
if his father had heard what Angelo said. He hoped he had not.
For, after all, was it his father's fault that there had been so few
sardines and that the salmon were hard to catch?

Angelo must have seen how his laughing hurt Nino, for he
stopped suddenly and began twirling his beautiful mustachios.
Then he gave Nino a little package of fresh herring for bait and
wished him good luck in his fishing.

Tony pushed his little rowboat away from the high dock that
stood above the water on great strong posts all ringed about
with white barnacles. Nino sat in the stern of the boat watching his father row with a long even pull on the oars. It was a
beautiful day now. The sky was very blue and there were no
clouds. Only big, gray-black sea gulls glided slowly up and
down the wind.

"They're waiting for the fine meal of fish tails they will get
when we come home," laughed Nino.

Suddenly there was a ripple on the quiet water and a
smooth brown head nosed up close to the little rowboat.

"Oh!" Nino jumped back a little. "Oh, it's the old sea lion!"

Tony stopped rowing. Nino took a herring from his package,
and threw it overboard. The sea lion wheezed, snuffling the
water. The brown head with the big brown eyes and long
whiskers rose up in the water, and Nino laughed and clapped
his hands as the great, lumbering sea lion caught the little fish
in mid-air. Then the brown head disappeared again. The water
ran off the smooth back and the tail flippers disappeared.

Tony chuckled as he started to row once more.

"Now he'll go back to his home under the docks and bark
at the tourists all morning teasing them to feed him."

The little fishing fleet was beginning to leave the harbor. The engines chugged softly around Tony's rowboat as it passed the DIANA, the TWO BROTHERS, the JENNY-N, and the TOMMY-BOY. Then Nino saw the SANTA ROSA, his father's boat, swinging at its mooring that looked like a great brown mushroom floating on the water. He could see how fresh it looked and he remembered how his father had spent all the time between the sardine months and the salmon months, scrubbing and painting his boat and getting her in order.

When the engine started its chug-chugging the SANTA ROSA gave a shiver all over as if she were as anxious as Nino to get started. Nino climbed the short ladder at the front of the boat and took hold of the round steering wheel. He must be ready to turn it as his father told him when Tony cast off from the mooring.

Now at last Nino felt the boat swing with the wind. They were soon out of the harbor. The SANTA ROSA followed the rest of the fleet as some went ahead and some came so close alongside that the men aboard called out to Tony.

"So, you have a new crew today, Tony. A fine helper, we see. Ah, what a lucky man! He will catch a big fish. Yes?"

They smiled at Nino as he stood proudly turning the wheel in his hand while his father tended the engine and soon started to bait the many hooks.

When they came to the fishing grounds where the best salmon ran, Nino watched the other boats until his father told him to turn. Then Tony made the engine go slowly. A soft "shug- a-shug." He swung the long outriggers away from the boat. Nino looked down and could see the bait, the sardines and the herrings go into the water. He knew his father would try first with the fish bait and if these did not catch anything then he would use the shiny metal "spoons" or "jigs" made of feathers. The six lines hanging from the long outriggers made little ripples as they moved slowly through the water.

Nino could hardly wait to get the fresh herring Angelo had given him onto his own hook, but he did not dare to leave the wheel until his father came up to take it. It seemed half the morning that Tony fussed with his lines and tinkered with the engines as if he had forgotten Nino waiting so impatiently at the wheel.

But at last Tony came up the ladder and Nino hurried to the stern. He picked up his long rod and, undoing the package of herring, he quickly had one of the little white fish dangling from his hook. Slowly he put it over the side, then unreeling the line, Nino let the water carry the fish far out behind the boat.

All the rest of the morning Nino waited and waited. He watched his own line. He watched his father's six lines trailing from the outriggers. But no salmon came. There were no tugs on Tony's lines. There was not even a nibble on Nino's fresh herring. He reeled in his line and put on some new bait. But no fish seemed to want it.

"Oh, please, salmon," Nino half whispered to himself. "Please salmon come up and hook yourself tight on my hook so that I can have a birthday party."

But no salmon came on his hook and only two came on Tony's lines.

The sun grew hot. Nino and Tony unwrapped their lunch that was done up in fresh newspaper. They sat together in the stern of the boat. Tony ate cheese and salami, but Nino ate only bread and an orange.

Nino felt sleepy. The sea was so shiny with all the sun. He was almost asleep when suddenly his line started to go. It went fast, the reel clicking as the line pulled away from it. Nino jumped up. How could he hold tight enough? Was this a whale? What could be swimming away so very fast with his line and his herring?

Nino knew how to play a fish. Tony had taught him. But what a fish this must be. Here he comes. No. Now away!

Swimming away. There—Nino saw him. There he was! A monster fish all right! Nino burst out laughing with excitement.

"Ho-ho, big fishy! Ho-ho, my fish! Come, come now! Slowly . . . slowly. There, forward . . . now back. Now I have you!"

Nino reeled in his line. He could feel now at last that the great fish was tired.

Slowly. Slowly. Then—quick to the side!

Tony reached far down in the water and hooked the fish with his long iron hook.

"Santa Maria!" cried Tony. "What a monster."

The great fish lay on the deck panting from the big fight with Nino. His gills went up and down. His tail flapped, flop, flop against the deck. The sun shone down on him, drying the water off his back. Nino could hardly believe his big fish.

No more salmon came to their lines that day. Soon the cold gray fog rolled in from the sea, and the far away fog horn blew "Whoo-oo." Then Tony knew it was time to go home. The other boats in the fleet turned, too. Like white ghosts they kept together chugging quietly through the gray fog into the harbor.

When Tony rowed his little boat back to the high dock once more, the other fisherman gathered about. They patted Nino on the back and Tony spoke proudly.

"Ah, what a party, Nino. What a wonderful party we will have. Fish, fish, fish! You can ask all your friends and we will have plenty to eat for everyone."

Suddenly Nino remembered what Angelo had said about fish for a party. Nevertheless he carried his great fish proudly up the dock. But he did hope that Angelo would be too busy inside his restaurant to see him go by. Nino did not want Angelo to tell his father that fish was no food for a party.

It was no use hoping, however, for just as Tony and Nino passed the pink door of the restaurant, it opened and Angelo himself came out. But he was only smiling, not laughing this time.

"Oh, what a little fisherman you have, Tony!" he called. Tony looked proudly at Nino and then at the great fish.

"Yes," he answered. "He has the biggest fish of the fleet today."

"I could use a fish like that." Angelo came close to Nino. "Yes, a fine, big, fresh fish like that is just what my customers like. How much do you want for it, Nino?"

"Oh," Tony answered quickly. "This fish is not for sale. Nino will have it for his birthday. We will have a big party with the fish, plenty of fish for everyone."

Nino did not dare look at Angelo. He was too afraid Angelo
would laugh at his father the way he had laughed at Nino and
tell him that fish was no food for a party.

But Angelo did not laugh. He didn't laugh at all. He was
just quiet for a moment. Then he said, "I'll tell you what we'll
do. You give me that fish for my customers and I'll give you a
birthday party at my restaurant."

Nino could hardly believe his ears. He, little Nino, to have a
birthday party at Angelo's! He hardly dared speak. But when
Angelo held out his hand, Nino gave him the fish.

"Fine! fine!" Angelo laughed very loud. "Now go and ask
everyone—every one of your friends."

"You mean," Nino said softly, "you mean as many as I
please?"

"Yes, yes, of course." Angelo smiled at him, rolling his mustachios into neat little points. "Tell them all to come. Tomorrow
night at Angelo's."

All the next day Nino went about asking people to his party.

He asked all his friends, the fishermen, and all their families.
He asked Mr. Anastasia the fish man.

He asked Piedro the barber, and Pierre the baker, who
always gave him stale cookies when he was hungry, and he
asked their wives and all their children.

He asked all his friends from school and especially his teacher,
because she was so pretty. When he got through, Nino could
not remember whom he had asked or how many—but everyone came!

The pink doors of Angelo's restaurant were wide open
and right in the middle of the front window, so that everyone
going by outside could see it, was Nino's fish. His great big,
beautiful fish. The wonderful fish that little Nino had caught
by himself.

It was all heaped about with cracked ice and decorated with
green parsley. Below it Angelo had put a sign:

Biggest fish of the day
CAUGHT BY NINO OF THE SANTA ROSA

Nino could hardly believe his eyes when he saw this and he could hardly believe his ears when he heard Angelo telling the tourists who wanted to come into his restaurant, "No, not tonight, but tomorrow. Come tomorrow and I will cook the big fish for you. Tonight I have invited only the little fisherman and his friends."

What a feast! There was soup and salad and antipasto. There was sausage and salami and pizza with anchovy. There was gnocchi and spaghetti with meat sauce. There was ravioli and hamburgers and hot dogs for those who preferred them. Then when this was all finished, there was silence!

"Oh-o-o!" gasped little Nino as Angelo himself came in from the kitchen carrying the most beautiful cake in the world. There were three layers, and on the very top was a great fish made of blue icing with seven candles sparkling in a circle around it.

It was all so gay and the cake was so beautiful that suddenly everyone began to sing and to dance, and they danced and they danced.

They even danced all the way home. All the way up the Fisherman's Wharf. All the way through the dark little streets and all the way to their houses. And little Nino never stopped dancing until at last he was tucked into bed.

Pick Me Up

BY WILLIAM JAY SMITH

Pick me up with a pile of blocks
And carry me past the Cuckoo Clocks!

Pick me up with a pile of hay
And carry me off to Buzzards Bay!

Pick me up with a pile of snow
And carry me out to Idaho!

Pick me up with a pile of twine
And carry me down to Argentine!

Pick me up with a pile of lava
And carry me over the hills of Java!

Pick me up with a pile of sand
And put me down in Newfoundland!

My Mother is the Most Beautiful Woman in the World

BY BECKY REYHER

Once upon a time, long, long ago, when the harvest season had come again in the Ukraine, the villagers were all busy cutting and gathering the wheat. For this is the land from which most Russians get the flour for their bread.

Marfa and Ivan went to the field early each day, as did all their children. There they stayed until sundown. Varya was Marfa's and Ivan's youngest little girl, six years old. When everyone went to the fields in harvest time, Varya went, too. Her legs were so short she had to run and skip to keep up with her mother's and father's long steps.

"Varyachka, you are a little slowpoke!" her father said to her. Then, laughing loudly, he swung her upon his shoulder, where she had to hold tight to his neck, for his arms were full carrying the day's lunch and the long scythe to cut the wheat.

In the field, in the long even rows between the thick wheat, Varya knew just what she must do. First, she must stay at least twenty or thirty paces behind her father, who now took even greater and bigger steps, so that he might have plenty of room to swing wide the newly sharpened scythe.

"Stand back, Varyachka! Mind the scythe!" her father warned. Swish, swish, swish, went his even strokes, and down came the wheat, faster and faster, as he made his great strides.

Soon Marfa began to follow Ivan. She gathered the wheat in sheaves or bunches just big enough to bind together with a strand of braided wheat. Varya, eager to be useful, helped gather the wheat, and held each bunch while her mother tied it. When three sheaves were tied, they were stacked against each other in a little pyramid.

"Careful, Varyachka!" her mother cautioned, "the wheat side up!"

After a while, instead of long rows of wheat, there were long rows of sheaves, standing stiffly.

Sometimes Varya forgot to follow her mother. On very hot days she stopped to rest upon the warm ground, and let her tired, bare feet and toes tickle the dark, moist earth. A while later she ran and caught up with her mother, and then her mother hugged her and wiped her dripping face. Even though her mother's arms and bosom were hot and damp, they felt cool and restful to Varya.

Day after day, Ivan, Marfa, and Varya went to the field until all the wheat was cut and stacked. Then a big wagon came and everyone pitched the wheat up to the driver who packed it in solidly, and carefully, and took it to the threshing barn.

When the harvest was over, Ivan, Marfa, Varya, and everyone in the village prepared for the feast day. And what a feast they had!

The villagers worked tirelessly throughout the summer. Their muscles ached, but there was a song in their hearts, and there were merry chuckles on their lips. Hard work produced a rich harvest. There would be wheat for everybody. It was time, then, for a grand celebration.

When Varya was five years old, a year ago, she was allowed to share in the excitement of preparing the feast. That summer she helped her mother bake little cakes stuffed with meat or cabbage. *Piroghki,* they were called.

The feast always took place after church in the very heart of the village. Varya came with her parents. Everybody was there. The grandmothers, whom Russians call *Baboushka,* and who always wear a gay kerchief tied below their chin. The mothers with babies in their arms. The strong broad-shouldered fathers. And the many children, all with roses in their cheeks.

Kolya, the village leader, played the accordion. The minute his music started, everybody's feet began to keep time. The boys whistled, and stamped their feet, and everybody clapped their hands.

Kolya stood in the center, all eyes upon him. He danced a jigging step or two, his fingers never leaving the accordion, and shouted: "Too quiet, my friends. A little more nonsense. A little more noise. A few more smiles. Sing! Sing! My friends, this is a holiday! Come! Everyone on their feet! We must have a dance!"

Men, women, and children joined in the singing, as Kolya swung his accordion into rollicking dance tunes.

The men wore polished, knee-high, heavy boots, but they danced as if their feet were bare. As the music grew faster and faster, their feet grew lighter and nimbler. It was as if the dancers had wings that carried them swiftly by those who were watching. To Varya it seemed that the older girls' braids flew by like birds in the wind.

The girls wore lots of petticoats under a skirt so wide you could not tell where it began, or where it ended. Around their necks were many strings of beads that shone as bright as a

Christmas tree, all tied with trailing strings of many-colored ribbons.

Some of the little girls were dressed almost as grandly. But not Varya, nor most of them.

Varya kept asking her mother: "When am I going to have a beautiful dance costume with lots of beads?"

And Varya's mother would say: "When you are a grown-up young lady, Varya."

Always it seemed to Varya she just could not wait until she was grown-up.

Varya was an impatient little girl. Her impatience was like a teasing toothache. Today it was so great she felt choked, as if she had swallowed a whole watermelon. For today was the last day for gathering the wheat. By evening all the wheat would be cut, stacked in pyramids, and waiting for the wagon to take it to the threshing barn. Tomorrow another wonderful feast day and celebration would come around again. Varya could hardly wait for the feast day to begin.

Bright and early Marfa, Ivan, and Varya went to the wheat field. "We must get to it," warned Ivan, "this is our last day to get the wheat in!"

"It has been a good crop, Ivan, hasn't it?" asked Marfa.

"Indeed, yes!" Ivan answered heartily, "And it will mean a good warm winter with plenty to eat. We have much to be thankful for."

Marfa and Ivan worked quicker and harder than ever. They did not seem to notice the hot sun.

But to Varya the day seemed the longest she had ever lived. The sun seemed hotter than on any other day, and her feet seemed almost too heavy to lift.

Varya peered into the next row of wheat which was not yet cut. There it was cool and pleasant and the sun did not bear down with its almost unbearable heat. Varya moved in just a little further to surround herself with that blessed coolness.

"How lucky I am!" she thought, "to be able to hide away from the hot sun. I will do this for just a few minutes. Surely Mamachka will not mind if I do not help her all the day."

Soon Varya grew sleepy, for in so cool a place, one could curl up and be very quiet and comfortable.

When Varya woke, she jumped to her feet and started to run toward her mother. But her mother was nowhere in sight.

Varya called, "Mama," "Mama," "Mamochka," but there was no answer.

Sometimes her mother got ahead of her and was so busy with her work she did not hear.

"Maybe if I run along the row, I will catch up with her," Varya thought.

She ran and ran, and soon she was out of breath, but nowhere could she see her mother.

"Maybe I have gone in the wrong direction," she said to herself. So she ran the other way. But here, too, there was no trace of her mother.

Varya was alone in the wheat fields, where she could see nothing but tall pyramids of wheat towering above her. When she called out, her voice brought no response, no help. Overhead the sun was not so bright as it had been. Varya knew that soon it would be night and that she must find her mother.

When it was almost dark, Varya stumbled into a clearing where several men and women had paused to gossip after the day's work. It took her only a second to see that these were strangers, and that neither her mother nor father were among them.

The little girl stared ahead of her, not knowing what to do. One of the men spied her and said in a booming voice which he thought was friendly, "Look what we have here!"

Everyone turned to Varya. She was sorry that with so many strangers looking at her, she had her hair caught back in a tiny braid with a bit of string, and that she was wearing only her oldest, most faded dress.

"Poor little thing," cried one of the women, putting her arms around Varya, "she is lost!" But this sympathy, and the strange voices made Varya want her mother all the more. She could not help crying.

"We must know her name, and the name of her mother and father. Then we can unite them," said the women.

"Little girl, little girl," they said, "what is your name? What is your mother's and father's name?" But Varya was too unhappy to speak.

Finally because her longing for her mother was so great, she sobbed out:

"My mother is the most beautiful woman in the world!"

All the men and women smiled. The tallest man, Kolya, clapped his hands and laughingly said, *"Now* we have something to go on."

This was long, long ago, when there were no telephones and no automobiles. If people wanted to see each other, or carry a message, they went on their two feet.

From every direction, friendly, goodhearted boys ran to village homes with orders to bring back the beautiful women.

"Bring Katya, Manya, Vyera, Nadya," the tall man, Kolya, called to one boy.

"Ay, but don't forget the beauty, Lisa," he called to still another boy.

The women came running. These were orders from Kolya, the village leader. Also the mothers, who had left the fields early to get supper for their families, thought perhaps this was indeed their child who was lost.

As each beautiful woman came rushing up, blushing and proud that she had been so chosen, Kolya would say to her: "We have a little lost one here. Stand back, everyone, while the little one tells us if this is her mother!"

The mothers laughed and pushed, and called to Kolya: "You big tease! What about asking each mother if this is her child? We know our children!"

To Varya this was very serious, for she was lost and she was desperate without her mother. As she looked at each strange woman, Varya shook her head in disappointment and sobbed harder. Soon every known beauty from far and near, from distances much further than a child could have strayed, had come and gone. Not one of them was Varya's mother.

The villagers were really worried. They shook their heads. Kolya spoke for them. "One of us will have to take the little one home for the night. Tomorrow may bring fresh wisdom to guide us!"

Just then a breathless, excited woman came puffing up to the crowd. Her face was big and broad, and her body even larger. Her eyes were little pale slits with a great lump of a nose between them. The mouth was almost toothless. Even as a young girl everyone had said, "A homely girl like Marfa is lucky to get a good husband like Ivan."

"Varyachka!" cried this woman.

"Mamochka!" cried the little girl, and they fell into each other's arms. The two of them beamed upon each other. Varya cuddled into that ample and familiar bosom. The smile Varya had longed for was once again shining upon her.

All of the villagers smiled thankfully when Varya looked up from her mother's shoulder and said with joy:

"This is my mother! I told you my mother is the most beautiful woman in the world!"

The group of friends and neighbors, too, beamed upon each other, as Kolya repeated the proverb so well known to them, a proverb which little Varya had just proved: *"We do not love people because they are beautiful, but they seem beautiful to us because we love them."*

Next day was the feast day. In the evening Varya sat cuddled in her mother's lap, and happily watched the dancing. As the music played she brought her mother's head close to her own and whispered: "Mamochka, the dancers, they are so beautiful. I love to watch them."

Her mother patted Varya and whispered back: "This is the harvest feast day. Everyone is wearing their best clothes, and their best smile. Of course it is fun to watch them!"

Varya was so happy and felt so safe, she was able to speak of the dark, awful moments when she was lost.

"Mamochka," she said, haltingly, as if she could not find the right words, "Some of the children have teased me. They laughed about my calling you the most beautiful woman in the world. They say the angels, the Czarina, the Princesses, the Queens, the rich, their own mothers, are the most beautiful. One of *them* is the most beautiful woman in the world."

"Mamochka," Varya went on, "I know that some of those women have more beads than you. Some have bigger and wider skirts. Maybe some of them can sing and dance better than you can. But, Mamochka, to me, you are the most beautiful woman in the world!"

Varya's mother, Marfa, kissed her, smiled happily and said: "Some people, Varyachka, see with their eyes alone. Others see with their hearts, too. I am grateful and lucky that you see with your heart, as well as with your eyes."

A. B. C. of Wheels

BY EVE MERRIAM

A

Airplane wheels fold up in the sky.

B

Baby-carriage wheels go bouncing by.

(Bye, baby, bye!)

C

Cement-mixer wheels clatter down the street.

D

Delivery wheels carry good food to eat.

E

Elevator wheels glide us up and down.

F

Fire engine wheels clang! clang! across town.

G

Garbage truck wheels grind up banana peels.

H

Hand truck looks like a ladder with two wheels.

I

Ice-cream-truck wheels bear a very sweet load.

J

Jeep wheels can jounce up the rockiest road!

K

Key-making wagon wheels move right along
While the key-maker man sings his key-making song:
   "Keys, please! I make keys!
   Not trees, not bees, not flies, and not cheese—
   But fine keys!"

L

Lawn-mower wheels clip, snip the green grass.

M

Motorcycle wheels rumble and roar as they pass.

N

Newspaper-truck wheels carry great paper stacks.

O

Oil-truck wheels carry hoses on their backs.

P

Pullman-train wheels click round and around.

Q

Quoits are wheels to toss on the ground.

R

Racing car wheels spin fast as thunder.

S

Steam-roller wheels roll gravel under.

T

Tractor wheels turn in meadows and plains.

U

Underground wheels for the subway trains.

V

Van wheels take furniture on moving day.

W

Wheelbarrows cart bricks and tools away.

X

Xmas tree truck wheels—guess what they bring?

Y

Yo-yo wheels slide up and down the string.

Z

Zoo-truck wheels carry sleepy polar bears,
Sleepy tall giraffes and sleepy little hares.

Now stand up like a pinwheel with your arms outspread,
And scoot like a wheel—right into bed!

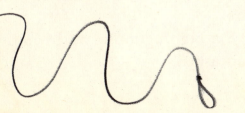

The Magic Whistle

BY ADÈLE AND CATEAU DE LEEUW

Michael walked along with his head down, not really seeing anything. A boy went by on a bicycle without using his hands, a cat was chasing her tail in the sunlight, a derrick was digging dirt out of a big hole behind a board fence, and a trash man was dumping cans into his red truck. But Michael didn't see or hear anything. He was thinking.

He was thinking how much he wanted a dog, and how long he had wanted a dog, and how just this morning his father and mother had both told him once again that he couldn't have one.

"A St. Bernard puppy costs at least one hundred and fifty dollars," his father had said. That was the kind Michael wanted, and it was true—they had been to the kennels and the man said a hundred and fifty dollars.

"And we'd have to have a big doghouse, and where would we put it?" his mother had asked.

"And the apartment's too small for a dog like that," his father had said.

"And he'd have to have so much meat that we couldn't afford it," his mother had put in.

Just the same, Michael wanted a dog—a St. Bernard with a heavy coat and big paws and wrinkles on his forehead and sad eyes. He'd hang a little keg on a cord around his neck and play that they were going to find a boy lost in the mountain snows, and he'd ride on his back as if he were a pony, and they'd romp together in the Park——.

Michael crossed into the Park and scuffed through the dead leaves. It was fall now, and he and his dog could have such good times playing together! He scuffed harder, because he felt his eyes getting wet. And just then his toes kicked against something.

It was little and hard, and at first he couldn't find it. But he scrabbled around in the leaves and finally discovered it. It was a piece of metal with a hole in it. It must be a whistle—though it didn't look like any whistle he had ever had.

He put it to his lips and blew. Not a sound came. Maybe it wasn't a whistle after all. But then, what was it? He blew harder and harder, till his cheeks puffed out and he got very red, but still no sound came. He screwed his eyes shut and blew till he thought he would burst.

When he ran out of breath, he opened his eyes. And he stared and stared, not able to believe what he saw.

For there, coming toward him, were dozens of dogs! Big dogs and medium-sized dogs and small dogs—smooth-haired and shaggy dogs, old and young dogs—red, black, white, gray, and brown dogs! They came running down the graveled path, they came scampering over the grass, they came bounding over the hill, they jostled each other and played around his feet, and barked, and leaped to his knees.

It was too good to be true. But it *was* true. There they were, clustered around him, looking up at him, wagging their tails, asking him what he wanted. And then he looked across the road and there, running lollopy-lollopy, was another dog—the littlest dog of all.

His body humped, his ears flopped, his tongue hung way out, and he seemed to say, "Wait for me, wait! I know I'm late, but I'm coming as fast as I can!"

A big dog jumped up and put his paws on Michael's shoulder and gave his face a lick. Michael saw that he had a little keg tied around his neck, and that he was a St. Bernard. On the keg was a tag and it said, "My name is Tor. . . . My home is 1295 Lake Street."

Then *he* couldn't be Michael's dog. He looked at the other dogs, and they had tags, too. "My name is Waldie. . . . I live at 102 George Street." "Binks. . . . If found, please return to Mrs. Holmes, Lane Apts."

Some of the dogs had run away again, but those that stayed all looked at him, as if they were asking, "Well, what are you going to do with us?" And he knew what he must do. He must return them to their owners. He knew how he would feel if he had a dog and his dog were lost or ran away.

"Come on," he said, and they followed him. It was hard taking care of so many. Some of them strayed off—into the Park, across a field, down a street. But he rang the bell at 1295 Lake Street and a lady came to the door.

"Tor!" she cried. "I thought you were lost!" And when Michael said he had found him in the Park, she gave him a quarter.

Then he took Waldie to his home, and the lady gave him fifty cents. Fifi's mistress hardly looked at Michael; she just grabbed Fifi and scolded her and shut the door. The man at Hans' house was very cross, and said Hans should know better and he had a good mind to make him do without his dinner.

Everywhere he went, the littlest dog lolloped beside him, his eyes sparkling, his tail wagging, his small furry feet scurrying over the ground.

One by one, Michael took the dogs home. Some people were glad, some were sad, some very angry, some were nice. Then, only the littlest dog was left. And the littlest dog had no tag. Michael didn't know where to take him.

He was very tired and sat down on the curb to think about what he would do.

"Don't you have any home?" he asked.

The littlest dog just looked up at him hopefully and licked at his finger tips.

Michael bent to pat him and the dog jumped up to lick his ear and cheek in a frenzy of delight.

"You aren't much like a St. Bernard," said Michael, "but there's something kinda cute about you. I wonder——"

Just then, a wagon pulled up beside him. The driver leaned out and asked sternly, "Whose dog is that?"

"He's—he's going to be mine," Michael said, swallowing hard.

"Where's his license? If he doesn't have a license, he goes to the pound." This must be the dog warden!

Michael opened his hand and showed the man the money. A dollar and a half! "I'm going to get a license now," he said. And he *would*—as soon as he had a chance.

"Well—see that you do," the man said gruffly and drove off.

Michael's heart went pound-pound, as he turned in at the apartment. The little dog lolloped beside him, eyes bright, tail wagging, and his father said, "Where have *you* been?" And his mother said, "What a sweet little dog!"

So Michael told about his adventure with the whistle and the dogs. He hunted in his pocket for the whistle, to show it to them, but it was gone.

"It must have been a dog whistle," his father said, laughing.

"But it didn't make a sound," Michael said.

"A whistle like that is called a Silent Dog Whistle," his father told him. "You can buy them in pet shops. They don't make a sound that *you,* or any human, can hear; they're too high. Just dogs can hear them. And when you blow one, a dog comes. Only you must have blown so long and so hard that *all* the dogs came."

Michael thought how wonderful that was. If only he had known before that there were such things as silent dog whistles! He looked down at Lollopy.

"May I keep this dog—may I?" Michael begged.

And his father said, "He'd need a very small doghouse."

And his mother said, "He wouldn't eat much."

And Michael said, "I love him."

"And I'm going to call you Lollopy," he told the little dog. Lollopy leaped into his lap and curled up, so he knew the name suited him.

Trees

BY HARRY BEHN

Trees are the kindest things I know,
They do no harm, they simply grow

And spread a shade for sleepy cows,
And gather birds among their boughs.

They give us fruit in leaves above,
And wood to make our houses of,

And leaves to burn on Hallowe'en,
And in the Spring new buds of green.

They are the first when day's begun
To touch the beams of morning sun,

They are the last to hold the light
When evening changes into night,

And when a moon floats on the sky
They hum a drowsy lullaby

Of sleepy children long ago . . .
Trees are the kindest things I know.

Eddie Goes to Dancing School

BY CAROLYN HAYWOOD

One day when Eddie came home from school his mother said, "Eddie, Mrs. Wallace was here this afternoon."

"You mean Toothless's mother?" Eddie asked.

"Eddie, that's a dreadful way to speak of Anna Patricia," said Mrs. Wilson.

"Well, it's true!" said Eddie. "She hasn't had any front teeth for such a long time that I guess she's never going to get any. And anyway, Anna Patricia is a silly name. Why don't they call her Anna or Patricia? Or just Pat? If I had a name like that I'd make everybody call me Pat."

"I guess Anna Patricia likes to be called by her full name," said Eddie's mother.

"Well, in school we all call her Toothless," said Eddie.

"Mrs. Wallace is forming a dancing class," said his mother. "She came to invite you to join."

Eddie looked at his mother with a face filled with horror. "A dancing class!" he cried. "What would I want to do that for?"

"Now, Eddie," said Mrs. Wilson, "it will be very nice for you to learn to dance. Dancing school is fun."

"Fun for the girls maybe, but not for boys. Are Rudy and the twins going?"

"It's just for the children in your room in school," said his mother.

"That's tough," said Eddie. Then his face brightened. "I know, Mama! You tell her Papa can't afford to send me to dancing school."

"But it's free, Eddie," said his mother. "Only the girls have to pay."

"That's a mean trick," said Eddie. "And I bet I'll have to dance with Toothless. And she lisps!"

"Of course you'll dance with Anna Patricia," said Mrs. Wilson. "The dancing class is going to be held at her home."

Eddie sat down and held his head. "Ugh!" he said "When?"

"Friday afternoon, at half past four," replied Mrs. Wilson.

"Friday afternoon!" wailed Eddie. "That's when we practice for the Saturday ball game."

"Eddie," said his mother, "you wouldn't want it to be on Saturday, would you?"

"Of course not," Eddie moaned. "But why does it have to be at all? Why do I have to learn to dance? Rudy and the twins don't have to learn to dance. Why do you pick on me?"

"Eddie, you will have a very nice time," said his mother. "Don't raise such a fuss. Go and see."

"If I don't like it can I stop?" Eddie asked.

"Yes, if you don't like it you can stop," his mother replied.

"O.K.!" said Eddie. "But don't tell Rudy and the twins that I have to go to dancing school."

"O.K.!" said Mrs. Wilson.

On Friday, when Eddie came home from school, his mother said, "Eddie, put on your best suit for dancing class."

"You mean my best Sunday suit?" said Eddie.

"Yes, dear," replied Mrs. Wilson.

"Golly! This dancing school business gets worse all the time," said Eddie.

Eddie washed his face and hands and soaked his hair with water. Then he took off his blue jeans and put on his best suit. "What will I do if I meet Rudy and the twins, all dressed up in my Sunday suit on Friday?" Eddie shrieked from his bedroom.

When he came downstairs his mother handed him a package. "These are your pumps, dear," she said.

"My what, Mama?" said Eddie, screwing up his nose.

"Your pumps," replied Mother, "your dancing pumps."

"What do I do with 'em?" Eddie asked.

"You wear them on your feet," said Mrs. Wilson.

"You mean I can't dance in my shoes?" Eddie cried.

"You would step on the little girls' feet, Eddie, in those clumsy shoes," said his mother.

"Serves 'em right!" said Eddie. "I'll walk all over Toothless's feet. Just let me at 'em."

"Eddie, do stop dawdling and get off." said his mother. "Have you money for bus fare? And don't forget to ask for a transfer."

Eddie pulled some change out of his pocket and looked at it. "O.K.," he said.

Just then he heard the twins coming in the front door. Eddie leaped like a deer and was out of the back door in a flash. He did not stop running until he reached his bus stop.

When the bus arrived Eddie stepped in. He knew the bus driver. He often rode with him. His name was Mike.

"Hi!" said Mike. "You look like a movie actor. All you need is a carnation in your buttonhole. Where you going, all dressed up?"

"Don't ask me," Eddie moaned. He flopped into the seat nearest the door.

"Come on, tell me. You'll feel better if you tell me," said Mike.

"You promise you won't tell anybody?" said Eddie.

"On my honor," said Mike.

Eddie got up and whispered in Mike's ear. "I'm going to dancing school. Isn't that horrible?"

"Oh! Cheer up!" said Mike. "I went to dancing school once. And look at me now."

"You did?" said Eddie, with a brighter face. He leaned over and whispered, "And did you have pumps?"

"Sure! Sure!" said Mike. "I was the best pumper in the crowd. You'll learn to pump. It's easy."

"No, Mike," said Eddie. "They're some kind of shoes. They're in this package."

"Oh, I thought that was your supper," said Mike. "Oh, sure! Pumps. Sure, you gotta have pumps."

"I have to change buses at Brewster Road," said Eddie.

"Righto!" said Mike. "Three more stops before we get there."

When the bus reached Brewster Road, Mike drew up to the curb. As Eddie stepped out he said, "So long, Mike."

"So long, pal!" said Mike. "I'll wait for you to cross the street."

Eddie crossed the street in front of the bus. When he reached the opposite corner, he heard Mike calling, "Hey, Eddie!"

Eddie looked back and saw a package flying toward him. It landed at his feet. "Your pumps," Mike called out, as he started the bus.

Eddie picked up the parcel and put it under his arm. He stood on the corner and waited for the other bus. Across the street there was a used car lot. It belonged to Mr. Ward, a friend of Eddie's father. Eddie looked over the cars while he waited. Suddenly, he caught sight of something bright red. Eddie's heart began to beat faster. He ran across the street and over to the lot. Sure enough! It was just what he thought. There was the fire engine he had ridden on at the Fair. A man was lying under it, working with a hammer.

Eddie stooped down and looked under. There was Mr. Ward. "Hello, Mr. Ward!" said Eddie. "I rode on this fire engine once. It was super!"

"You did, Eddie!" said Mr. Ward, pushing himself out from between the wheels. "Well, how would you like to ride on it again?"

"Now?" said Eddie, his eyes shining.

"I want to see how it runs," said Mr. Ward. "I just put in a new part."

"Swell!" said Eddie, climbing right up into the front seat. "This is great!" he added, as the fire engine started.

Then Mr. Ward looked down on the ground. "Does that bundle belong to you?" he asked.

"Oh, golly! Yes," said Eddie. "Stop."

The fire engine stopped and Eddie got down. He ran back and picked up his package. Then he climbed up again. He put the package on the seat beside him and they started off. "I sure like this fire engine," he said.

"You going anywhere special?" Mr. Ward asked.

"Oh, not very special," Eddie replied.

"Got plenty of time?" said Mr. Ward.

"Oh sure!" said Eddie.

"Very well! She's going good. We'll take a spin around," said Mr. Ward.

Eddie held onto the seat and swung his legs. This was wonderful! "Can I pull the bell?" he asked.

"No, we can't ring the bell," said Mr. Ward. "The fire company would object. Might look like a false alarm."

Mr. Ward drove Eddie way out into the country before he said, "I guess I had better get back. Where can I drop you?"

Eddie thought of dancing school for the first time since he had been on the bus. "Oh! I have to go to Beech Tree Road," he said.

"Beech Tree Road?" said Mr. Ward. "What's going on there? By the way, you look all slicked up."

"Yeah," said Eddie. "I forgot all about it. I'm going to dancing school."

"You don't say!" said Mr. Ward. "What have you got in the package?"

Eddie looked sheepish. "Aw, pumps," he said.

"Pumps!" said Mr. Ward. "What the heck are pumps?"

"I don't know," said Eddie. "Something you wear on your feet."

"Well, suppose I take you right over to the place," said Mr. Ward.

"Oh, that would be great!" said Eddie.

Mrs. Wallace was standing at the front door when Eddie drove up in the fire engine. As he jumped down she said, "Why, Eddie! You're very late. I've been wondering why you didn't get here."

"I guess I am a little late," said Eddie. "Mr. Ward gave me a lift."

Eddie could hear the boys and girls laughing. They were all in the dining room.

"It's too bad you missed the dancing class," said Mrs. Wallace. "The children are having their ice cream now."

Eddie's face shone. "Ice cream?" he said. "Gee, that's great!"

"Hello, Eddie!" the children called out when Eddie walked into the dining room.

"Hello!" said Eddie, sitting down at the table.

Mrs. Wallace handed him a large plate of ice cream and Eddie lost no time in eating it. Just as he swallowed the last spoonful, the doorbell rang. Mrs. Wallace went to the front door and opened it. Eddie heard Mr. Ward's voice say, "Is Eddie Wilson still here?"

"Yes, he is," said Mrs. Wallace.

"Well, here are his pumps," said Mr. Ward.

The children had caught a glimpse of the fire engine through the open door. They rushed to the door to look at it. "Oh, here's the fire engine that was at the Fair!" they cried.

"I had a ride on it this afternoon," said Eddie.

"Oh, can we have a ride?" the children shouted. "Can we have a ride?"

"You have on your best clothes," said Mrs. Wallace. "You can't go riding on a fire engine in your best clothes, in your dancing clothes."

"We won't hurt them," the children cried.

"I didn't hurt mine, did I?" said Eddie.

"I'll take them all home," said Mr. Ward.

The children rushed to the fire engine, the little girls in their ruffled dresses and the boys in their Sunday suits.

"Now, everybody sit still," said Mr. Ward. "You have to keep your clothes clean."

Just as everyone was settled Eddie jumped down. "Wait a minute," he said.

He ran into the house and came back with his package. He looked up at Mr. Ward and grinned. "Forgot my pumps," he said.

Mr. Ward dropped the children off, one by one. Eddie was the last. When he drove up to the house, the twins were looking out of the window. When they saw Eddie, they rushed to the front door.

"What's the idea," cried Joe, "riding on the fire engine?"

"Where have you been?" cried Frank.

"I've been to dancing school," said Eddie.

"Dancing school!" cried the twins in chorus.

"Gee, it's swell!" said Eddie, as he waved good-by to Mr. Ward.

When dinner was almost over, the doorbell rang. Mr. Wilson went to the door and opened it and everyone around the dining-room table heard Mr. Ward's voice say, "Here are Eddie's pumps. He left them on the fire engine."

When Mr. Wilson came back to the dining room, he was carrying a package. He put it on the window sill. "Here are your pumps, Eddie," he said.

"Pumps!" cried Rudy and the twins together. "What are pumps?"

"I don't know," said Eddie. "I haven't had time to look at 'em. But dancing school was swell, Mama. Dancing school was swell!"

Why Cowboys Sing in Texas

BY LE GRAND HENDERSON

Everybody knows how cowboys sing today in Texas.
    But there was a time when cowboys did not sing in Texas.
That was a lonely time.
    This story tells how song came to Texas.
    This is the story heard beside a campfire by the Rio Grande.
The story of why cowboys sing today in Texas.

    Today cowboys sing in Texas.
    They sing, "Yippee yi."
    And they sing, "Yippee yay."
    Everybody knows how cowboys sing today in Texas.
    But it was not always so.
    Things were quiet once in Texas.

Long ago, in the days when cowboys did not sing.

Cowboys were silent then.

And the most silent cowboy in all of Texas was Slim Jim Bean.

Once, in that old and silent time, Slim Jim was guarding a herd of cattle at night.

It was a long dark night. And Slim Jim Bean was lonely.

I wish I could hear a little noise, he thought. Any kind of a little noise that would not frighten the cows.

Slim Jim knew that if anything frightened the cows they would stampede. They would stampede and run all over Texas. It might take a month of Sundays to round them up again.

Slim Jim thought of just the noise he would like to hear. It was a song he sang when he was a boy. He remembered the words. He remembered the tune.

"I believe I could sing that song again," he said. "Just a little song should not frighten the cows."

So Slim Jim opened his mouth and he sang.

The song woke the cows. And they didn't like it. They couldn't stand that song.

A big black cow stampeded.

A little yellow cow stampeded.

Big ones and little ones, spotted ones and plain ones—they all stampeded. They stampeded all over Texas.

Slim Jim and the other cowboys rode out to round up the cows.

They rode through the mesquite with its long straight thorns.

They rode through the Spanish dagger with its long sharp spikes.

They rode through the cat's-claw with its long curved briers.

And they rode through clumps of cactus with its long prickly needles.

But the thorns did not hurt them. And the spikes did not hurt them. And the briers did not hurt them. And the needles did not hurt them. Because they wore leather cowboy chaps on their legs.

Slim Jim was the best rider and the best roper in all Texas. But it took him and the other cowboys half a month of Sundays to round up those cows.

"Now, listen!" the other cowboys said to Slim Jim. "No more singing in Texas."

And Slim Jim promised he would sing no more.

He would sing no more in Texas.

That night Slim Jim went out to guard the cows again.

It was very quiet, and Slim Jim was lonely. He thought about his song. The song kept running through his mind.

Slim Jim tried to keep his promise. He tried hard not to sing. But the song went round and round in his mind. It went round and round. It went round and round.

Slim Jim couldn't hold it back. He opened his mouth and he sang his song.

And the cows didn't like it.

A little tan cow stampeded.

A big red cow stampeded.

Big ones and little ones, spotted ones and plain ones—they all stampeded. They stampeded all over Texas.

Slim Jim and the other cowboys had to ride through all those thorny bushes again.

This time it took them nearly a whole month of Sundays to round up these cows.

"Now listen!" the other cowboys said to Slim Jim. "There will be no more singing. No more singing in Texas."

"Boys," Slim Jim said, "I can't promise. It's lonely at night on this lone prairie. That song keeps running through my mind. It goes round and round. It goes round and round. And when that happens, I have to sing it."

Then Slim Jim got on his horse and he said, "I can't promise not to sing. So I will go away. I will go far away. I will find a

place where there are no cows to be frightened by my singing."
And Slim Jim rode away.

On the tenth day Slim Jim came to a river. It was a very
dry river. It was so dry that it was dusty. So Slim Jim knew it
was the Rio Grande. Everyone in Texas knows the Rio Grande
is the dustiest river in the world.

There was a little water out in the middle. But not enough
for the fish to swim in. They had to walk on the bottom.

Slim Jim could see them walking around down there.

"Hm," he said, "a tasty fish would make a fine supper."

Slim Jim was a cowboy, not a fisherman. He had no fishhooks
and he had no fishline.

But Slim Jim saw something. He saw that there was only
enough river to cover the smallest fish. The biggest ones were
half out of water as they walked along the bottom.

Slim Jim was a cowboy and he was a good roper. He was
the best roper in all Texas. So he whirled his rope——

And he roped a fish.

Slim Jim camped on the riverbank and cooked his fish.

It was lonely there, besides the river. Slim Jim's song kept
running through his mind. He opened his mouth and he sang.
He sang that song. And his song did not frighten the fish in the
Rio Grande. Not a single fish stampeded.

"This is the place for me," Slim Jim said. "I shall stay here,
and sing, and be a fisherman."

So Slim Jim laid aside his leather cowboy chaps, because a
fisherman would not need them. And he stayed beside the
river. And he fished. And he sang.

But while Slim Jim fished and sang there was trouble in
Texas.

The other cowboys remembered Slim Jim's song. That song
kept running through their minds. It went round and round.
It went round and round.

They just couldn't help it—they sang that song.

And the cows didn't like it. They couldn't stand that song.

A big brown cow stampeded.

A little white cow stampeded.

Big ones and little ones, spotted ones and plain ones—they all stampeded. They stampeded all over Texas.

The cowboys rode for a whole month of Sundays. But they couldn't get the cows rounded up again.

Then up spoke Cactus Pete of the Pecos country.

"Boys," he said, "we need help. Slim Jim Bean is the best cowboy in all Texas. We must get Slim Jim to help us round up those cows."

The other cowboys agreed.

So they rode out to find Slim Jim.

They rode all over Texas. They rode until they came to the Rio Grande River.

And that was where they found Slim Jim, fishing.

"Cows are stampeding all over Texas, Slim Jim," they told him. "We must get them rounded up again or Texas will be plumb ruined. You must help us round up those cows, Slim Jim."

Slim Jim turned away from the river.

His voice rose loud and free.

"Slim Jim will ride and round 'em up," he cried. "All you cowboys follow me."

So Slim Jim rode to round up the cows. The cows that were stampeding all over Texas.

He rode through all those thorny bushes.

And Slim Jim felt the thorns. He felt them because he was not wearing his chaps. The leather cowboy chaps he laid aside when he became a fisherman.

When he felt the mesquite thorns, Slim Jim shouted, "Yip!"

When he felt the Spanish dagger spikes, Slim Jim shouted, "Yippee!"

When he felt the cat's-claw briers, Slim Jim shouted, "Yi!"
When he felt the cactus needles, Slim Jim shouted, "Yay!"
And when he felt them all at the same time, Slim Jim shouted,
"Yippee yi, yippee yay!"

Slim Jim rode through all the thorny bushes in Texas. And
his voice rose loud and free, "Yippee yi, yippee yay!"

Everywhere that Slim Jim rode, the cows heard him. The
cows that were stampeding all over Texas. They liked those new
sounds that Slim Jim made. They stopped running to listen to
Slim Jim's yips and yippees and yis and yays.

Then up spoke Cactus Pete of the Pecos country.

"Slim Jim," he said, "the cows like those yippee-yi noises."

The other cowboys all said, "Make those noises again, Slim
Jim. The yippee-yi noises. The noises the cows like."

So Slim Jim did it. He made the noises again. And he made
them again. He made a song out of those noises.

Yippee yi, yippee yay—yippee.

The other cowboys listened. They liked Slim Jim's new song.
So they all joined in and sang.

The cows liked the new song.
The big cows liked it.
The little cows liked it.
Big ones and little ones, spotted ones and plain ones—they
all stopped to listen.
Then Slim Jim and the other cowboys rounded them up.
And that was the end of the big stampede, in Texas.

And that is why cowboys sing today in Texas.
They sing, "Yippee yi."
And they sing, "Yippee yay."
They sing Slim Jim's song today in Texas.

The Lucky Number

BY CATHERINE WOOLLEY

It was a lovely Saturday morning in June. Billy and his little sister Letty were hurrying along the street.

They were going to a big party for the school children, to celebrate the end of school. The party was in the school stadium.

Billy had been up extra early, to be sure to get there on time. Letty had been up early, too.

"You can go with me, Letty," Billy had told her, "even if you don't go to school."

"That's a good boy," Mother had said with a smile.

Billy took Letty's hand as they went along. He quickened his step.

"Walk faster, Letty!" he said.

They were not late. There was a long line at the stadium gate.

"Hi, Billy!" That was Jimmy, a boy in Billy's class. "Want to play marbles while we're waiting?"

"Sure!" Billy said. "You stand right here, Letty."

Billy kept his eye on Letty while he played marbles. Letty was watching something farther up in the line.

The line began to move faster. Jimmy put his marbles in his pocket. Billy and Jimmy went back to their places.

Now Billy saw what Letty was looking at. She was looking at a doll that a little girl was carrying. She couldn't keep her eyes off the doll.

Letty looked at her brother. "I'm going to get a doll like that for my birthday!" she said.

Billy said nothing. Mother and Daddy worked hard. But they did not have enough money to buy Letty a big doll. Billy was afraid Letty would be disappointed.

Now, they were at the stadium gate. A man handed Billy a paper bag and a ticket. He handed Letty a paper bag and a ticket.

"Keep your tickets," the man called. "You may have a lucky number."

Billy held Letty's hand tightly. They climbed the steps to the seats and sat down.

Quickly, children filled the seats.

"Look, Letty," Billy said. "There's candy in your bag."

He opened the bag for her. It held small hard candies. Billy and Letty sat happily eating their candy.

A band played. They all stood up to sing "The Star Spangled Banner."

The entertainment began. On a platform down on the field, a man juggled balls. He kept five balls spinning in the air at once. The children cheered.

A man climbed on another man's shoulders and stood on the man's head. The children liked that too.

Soon, the entertainment was over.

Now a man stood on the platform and spoke through a microphone.

"We're going to read the lucky numbers," he said. "Prizes are only for school children."

Billy thought, "Letty can't win a prize. She won't go to school until fall."

A girl on the platform put her hand into a box and took out a ticket.

"The first lucky number," the man called, "is 106. One, oh, six. Whoever has 106 please come and get this fine prize."

He held up the prize. It was a brand-new baseball bat.

Billy looked down at his number. Number 85. "Oh," he thought. "if I could only win a baseball bat!"

A boy ran down the steps and across the field to the stage. He gave the man his ticket. The man handed him the baseball bat.

"Oh-h-h!" said all the children loudly. The boy came smiling back to his seat, carrying the bat.

The man held up a fuzzy toy dog. He read the lucky number. A girl had the number. She brought back the toy dog.

Then a boy won a cowboy hat.

"I wish I had a hat like that," Billy thought.

A girl won a huge rubber ball.

A boy won a baseball.

"Gee, but I'd like a baseball," Billy thought.

The man held up the next prize. It was a big doll with light curly hair and a pink dress.

"Here is a fine prize!" the man called. "Does some lucky little girl have the lucky number? The number is 85—eight, five."

Billy's heart gave a jump. He looked quickly at the ticket clutched in his hand. It was 85 all right!

"I've got it!" he cried, jumping up.

The boys around him began to laugh and hoot.

"Ha, ha! See who gets the doll!" one boy said.

"Hey, go get your dolly!" another one called.

"Look who plays with dolls, fellows!" shouted a third.

Billy sat down again.

If he went to the platform and carried back the doll, all the boys in the stadium would laugh. He couldn't do it.

Then he saw Letty. She was sitting on the edge of her seat. Her brown eyes were fastened on the doll.

For a moment, Billy sat there.

"Who has 85?" the man called. "Who wins this beautiful doll?"

Slowly, Billy got up. He went down the steps. He walked across the field.

In the seats the children began to laugh and whistle.

Billy climbed the steps to the platform. He held out his ticket.

"Eighty-five," the man read. "Tell the lady here your name and school."

Then the man looked at Billy. "Suppose we give you a baseball bat instead of the doll, son," he said.

Billy's heart leaped up.

Then he thought how much Letty wanted a doll.

Billy looked at the baseball bat. He looked at the doll. He took a deep breath.

"No, thanks," he said. "I'll take the doll."

He marched down the steps carrying the big doll.

Again the children whistled and laughed to see Billy carrying the doll. Billy looked straight ahead.

He was halfway to his seat when Letty came running to meet him.

Billy stopped. He gave the doll to Letty. He took Letty's hand. Together, they climbed back to their seats.

The laughing and whistling died down.

Then, all through the stadium, the children began to clap their hands. They clapped them long and loud for Billy.

Lights

BY CLAUDIA LEWIS

Sparkle! Glisten!
Come and listen
To this story of sparkling things,
Of light and fire and golden rings.

All people on the earth love glittering things.
They wear bright jewels and bracelets and rings,
They sit about the fire, and stare
At the sparkle there.
They love brooks that winkle in the sun,
And lakes that crinkle—
(Water's no fun on a day that's grey.)

And think of the night
Sparkling with light!
People come from far away
And stay up late at the top of the Empire State
To look at the sight—
New York City lighted at night.

People on planes twenty thousand feet high
In the dark sky
Look down when they pass over a lighted town.
"It lies there like a jewel," they say,
Speaking to each other, though they are strangers.
And they watch, and watch,
Until the plane has flown away.

People love the glittering stars—
All people, whether they are children or astronomers.

And they love all other little sparks of light—
Candle flames,
Match fires,
A little flashlight in the night,
Cats' eyes burning bright,
Any eyes that shine—
Yours and mine—
    (They even love glass stars, and sew them
    on cowboy belts and evening dresses.)

People love a sunny summer day—
In the country, the leaves of trees flicker in the sun
Like a million little dimes twinging in the breeze.
In the city, bright daytime stars
Sparkle from the metal on all the parked cars.

People love the lights of Christmas—
"Oh Christmas tree," they say,
"And Christmas time—stay! stay!"

They love the Fourth of July
With skyrockets bursting in the sky,

And Hallowe'en night
When pumpkins shine
With candlelight.

And of course they love that brightest spark of all,
That giant pumpkin shining in the sky,
That warm and yellow light a-burning—

    The Sun,

That star of ours,
That shines down on this world so gently turning.

The White Horse

BY ALICE M. DALGLIESH

Once there was a white horse that always stayed in the same place. He never galloped or walked or trotted. He never neighed and he never nickered. He did not eat oats and he did not eat hay. And this was because the horse was a wooden horse.

The white horse stood outside a shop that was painted red. A sign over the door of the shop said:

HARNESS MAKER

Some days the white horse wore a set of harness to show what fine harness could be bought in the shop.

Every spring Mr. Bobbins, who was the harness maker, gave

the white horse a bright new coat of paint. Always on a sunny day in April Mr. Bobbins came out with a large pot of white paint and a large paintbrush. Then he began to paint the horse.

It was not long before all the children began to gather. They loved to watch Mr. Bobbins paint. Up and down, up and down went the paintbrush, and the white horse became whiter and whiter.

"Please, Mr. Bobbins, may I have the brush just a minute? Please, may I paint? Please, Mr. Bobbins?"

Sometimes Mr. Bobbins let the very careful children paint, but he only let them paint the insides of the white horse's legs, and other places that did not show.

One spring Mr. Bobbins was very sad. It seemed that not enough people were buying harness, and so the shop would have to close. What would become of the white horse?

"I can't bear to sell him," said Mr. Bobbins. "What shall I do with him?" He thought and thought, and then he put up a sign which said:

THE WHITE HORSE WILL

BE GIVEN TO THE PERSON

WHO CAN GIVE HIM

THE BEST HOME

ONE WEEK ON TRIAL

Such excitement as there was in the little town! Everyone wanted the horse. First of all the veterinary took him.

"He will make a grand sign for me, and he can stand right on my front lawn," he said. So he put the horse on his front lawn and around his neck he hung a sign which said:

J. TOPPER, *Veterinary*

But after a week Mr. Bobbins took the horse back again. "The idea of letting him stand in the boiling sun and blister his white coat!" he said.

So the white horse went to the barber, who allowed little boys to ride on him before they had their hair cut. The trouble was that bad little boys who did not want to have their hair cut kicked the white horse, and kicked some of the white paint off of him.

"That will never do," said Mr. Bobbins, and he took the horse back again. The white horse went to seven homes, but none of them was just right; and at the end of each week, there he was back in the yard of Mr. Bobbins's house, under a shady tree where his paint would not blister.

"Whatever shall I do with him?" asked Mr. Bobbins. He had to go away on a business trip, so he said to Mrs. Bobbins, "I am going to be away for two whole months. Now, whatever you do, take good care of the white horse."

"I certainly shall," said Mrs. Bobbins.

Mr. Bobbins was away for two whole months, and when he came back he said to Mrs. Bobbins, "Did you take good care of the white horse?"

"I certainly did," said Mrs. Bobbins. "Go see for yourself."

Mr. Bobbins stepped out into the back yard. What he saw made him stand perfectly still, with his hair standing on end. There was the white horse. But Mrs. Bobbins, who loved flowers, had planted a garden around him. Marigolds grew around his feet, and tall hollyhocks leaned against his white sides. Worst of all, blue morning-glories twined in his tail and scrambled around his neck.

"Isn't he a lovely sight?" asked Mrs. Bobbins.

"A lovely sight indeed!" Mr. Bobbins almost burst. "An insult to a fine horse! Morning-glories climbing all over him. An insult, I say!"

He untwined the morning-glories while Mrs Bobbins looked sadly on and wiped her eyes on her apron.

"There's no pleasing some people," she said. "I'm sure I don't know what you're going to do with him unless—unless you give him to the new playground."

"What playground?" asked Mr. Bobbins.

Then Mrs. Bobbins said that the town had opened a new playground for the children. "I think they'd like to have the horse," she said. "Maybe he's a little too tall for the children to ride on, but you could hitch him up to that old sleigh that's been standing in the barn for years."

"The very thing," said Mr. Bobbins. He kissed his wife on both her rosy cheeks. "You do have good ideas," he said, "and I do forgive you about the morning-glories. Of course, you couldn't know how a fine horse like that would feel about morning-glories."

"They were the *best* morning-glories," said Mrs. Bobbins. "Heavenly Blue."

"That makes no difference," said Mr. Bobbins. "The idea is the same. Here, let's look at the sled."

It was not long before the sled was out in the yard, being painted a bright and beautiful green. It was a proud day for Mr. Bobbins when the sled and the horse were loaded on a wagon and taken up to the playground. Mr. Bobbins himself chose the place where they were to stand, under a shady tree so that the paint would not blister. They really did look very handsome, the white horse and the green sled. The townspeople put a little sign on the sled which said:

PRESENTED TO

THE PLAYGROUND BY

B. BOBBINS

Mr. Bobbins was very proud. Twice a week he went up to the playground to watch the children play in the sled.

"Get up, horse!" the children would say, shaking the reins. "Here we go!"

And Mr. Bobbins would smile. "That's the life for a fine white horse!" he said. "Yes, that's the life!"

Mrs. Moodle and the Tea-tray

BY ROSE FYLEMAN

I wonder whether any of you remember Mrs. Moodle and her poodle, Troodle, and her funny maid, Boodle?

Well, in case you don't, I must remind you that Mrs. Moodle was a very nice, comfortable old thing, who wore a dress made of lovely shiny black satin with little frills all the way up, and a bonnet with a pink rose in it. And she always carried an umbrella. *Now* do you remember?

Well, one morning Mrs. Moodle was reading her paper, and this is what she saw:

> Why go abroad for winter sports? You
> can enjoy all the thrills of tobogganing
> in your own home by sliding down the
> stairs on a tea-tray.

"What a wonderful idea," said Mrs. Moodle. "I shall certainly try it at once."

So Boodle was told to bring the tin tray from the kitchen dresser. It was a very nice tray with a gold border all round it.

"Why go abroad for winter sports, Boodle?" said Mrs. Moodle.

"I'm sure I don't know, Mum," said Boodle.

"That's just it, Boodle," said Mrs. Moodle. "Give me the tea-tray."

Mrs. Moodle spent a delightful morning tobogganing down the stairs. The stairs went from the first floor into the hall in one perfectly straight flight. I don't know how many times she climbed up and tea-trayed down. She seemed to get quicker and quicker at it. Boodle was in the kitchen; she couldn't be persuaded to have a go, but she could hear Mrs. Moodle arrive each time with a bump on the rug at the foot of the stairs and slide across the hall.

She slid right up to the front door.

Boodle was so busy listening to the bumps that she never heard the front doorbell, which rang in the scullery. Mrs. Moodle didn't hear it either. She was far too excited. Once, twice, it rang.

Then the person on the doorstep grew impatient.

He turned the handle. The door opened, and he came forward into the hall. And just at that moment Mrs. Moodle came flying down the stairs on her tea-tray.

"Look out!" she yelled. But it was too late.

She dashed, tea-tray and all, right into the legs of the stranger who had come in, and sent him sprawling on to his back.

He picked himself up and Mrs. Moodle picked *herself* up and neither of them spoke for a minute.

The stranger was too annoyed and astonished to speak, I think. Mrs. Moodle was too confused.

At last the stranger found his voice.

"Are you Mrs. Moodle?" he gasped.

"Yes," said Mrs. Moodle.

"Well, I never," said the stranger. And he turned round and walked out of the front door and was never seen again.

Boodle says she's sure he was Mrs. Moodle's long-lost cousin from Australia who had come to give her half his fortune. He had a little black bag, which she says they always have.

Mrs. Moodle sometimes wonders whether he *was* a long-lost cousin. But he's never come back.

The Bottle That Went To Sea

BY LILIAN MOORE

One day Jimmy's mother got a letter. She read the letter to Jimmy. This is what the letter said:

Dear Mrs. Jones;
Yes, you may have the little brown house on Little White Beach. You may live in it all summer.

"All summer!" said Jimmy. "Will we live at a beach all summer?"

"Yes," said his mother, and you could see she was happy too.

"When will we go?" asked Jimmy. He did not see how he could wait.

"Soon," said his mother.

Soon? How many days was that? It seemed a long, long time to Jimmy.

Then one day his mother and father began to pack. Jimmy helped, too. They packed boxes and bags. Bags and boxes. They all went into the car.

And off went Jimmy and his mother and father to the little brown house on the beach.

As soon as they got there, Jimmy ran out to play. He played in the sand. He found shells. He found a starfish. He splashed in the water.

"Oh, I like it here!" he said. "I like it here on Little White Beach."

He played the next day, too. He played in the sand. He splashed in the water. He found more shells, and another starfish.

He played the day after that, and the day after that. Then he looked around. He looked at the sea. He looked at the sand.

But Jimmy did not feel happy.

He ran back to the little brown house.

"Mother," he said, "there's no one to play with here."

"There will be soon," said his mother. "We came here a little early. There will be other children here soon."

Soon? How many days was that? Soon always sounded as if it would be right away. But it often seemed like a long, long time.

Jimmy walked slowly out to the beach.

He wanted to dig a deep, deep hole and fill it with water, but it was no fun to do it alone.

He wanted to build a big, big, BIG sand castle. But it was hard to do it alone.

He stood and looked at the sea.

All at once, Jimmy saw something bobbing around in the water.

It came closer and closer.

Jimmy pulled it in. It was a bottle. A little green bottle with a cork in it.

A bottle floating in from the sea!

Jimmy thought about a story he once heard. In the story, a man on a big boat threw a bottle into the sea. There was a letter in the bottle. The bottle sailed far away with the letter.

Jimmy ran into the house. "Mother," he said, "will you please write a letter for me to put in this bottle."

This is what the letter said:

To the one who finds this bottle:
My name is Jimmy Jones. I am six years old. I live on Little White Beach in a little brown house.

Then Jimmy put the letter into the bottle, and pushed the cork back in. He ran down to the beach with the bottle, and threw it as far as he could, far into the sea.

"Have a good trip!" Jimmy laughed, as he watched the bottle float away, out with the sea.

"Maybe it will be picked up by a big liner at sea!" thought Jimmy.

Maybe someone far out on a fishing boat would pick it up and read the letter. Maybe someone in a tug boat out at sea would find it first.

Maybe it would sail on and on till it went all around the world!

Jimmy watched his bottle till he could not see it any more.

The little bottle did sail away as the sea went out.

But that night, when the sea came in again, it carried the bottle back to the beach. Not to Little White Beach, but to another little beach not far away, called Sandy Shore.

The next morning a boy was walking along the beach at Sandy Shore.

He picked up the little green bottle and saw there was a letter inside.

He ran to his house.

"Mother," he said, "look, there's a letter inside this bottle! Will you please read it to me?" His mother read the letter:

> *To the one who finds this bottle:*
> *My name is Jimmy Jones. I am six years old. I live on Little White Beach in a little brown house.*

"Hooray!" cried the boy. "Hooray! At last there's a boy around here I can play with!"

Then he said, "Mother, may I go over to Little White Beach? I know where the little brown house is."

"Why, yes," said his mother. "It's not very far. And ask Jimmy Jones if he wants to come and play here, too."

Off ran the boy with the little green bottle. Off to Little White Beach.

Jimmy was playing in the sand. He was wishing again that he could make a big, big sand castle.

"Hi" said someone behind him.

Jimmy looked around.

There was a boy looking at him. "Hi!" said the boy again. "I found your bottle with the letter in it!" He held out the bottle to Jimmy.

"You did?" cried Jimmy. "Where did you find it?"

"Right down there," said the boy, and he showed Jimmy. "Right at the next beach where I live. I came over to play."

Jimmy laughed.

So his bottle had not gone far away. No big liner had picked it up. No man on a fishing boat had seen it. No tug boat out at sea had found it. No one across the world had read his letter.

Better than all that—another boy he could play with had found it!

"How would you like to build a sand castle?" he asked his friend.

And they began to build a big, big, BIG sand castle—the kind that only two boys can make when they build together.

Bertram's Trip to the Moon

BY PAUL T. GILBERT

"What's that you're making, Bertram?"

Ginny Banning had clumped across the lawn on her roller skates to where Bertram was busy with his saw and hammer. He had nailed some old bedsprings to the bottom of an empty flour barrel, and now was sawing a little door in the side of the barrel.

Bertram didn't even look up. He kept on sawing. Girls, he thought, always wanted to know everything, especially Ginny Banning.

Ginny waited for a moment and then said, "A chicken coop?"

"A chicken coop! Good night!" said Bertram. "That just goes to show how much girls know about it."

"A doghouse then," said Ginny.

But Ginny was wrong again. She would never, in a thousand years, have guessed what it was that Bertram was making out of that barrel.

A spaceship! A rocket which would take him to the moon.

"Oh!" said Ginny when Bertram finally answered her question. "Can I go too?"

"There wouldn't be room for both of us," said Bertram. "And besides, you'd be afraid."

"Oh, I would, would I?" She made a face at Bertram. Hadn't she ridden with him on a winged horse through the clouds in a thunderstorm? Hadn't she been chased by a wild rhinoceros? Scared? Not Ginny Banning.

All Ginny said though was, "When are you going to start?"

"As soon as I finish my spaceship—if I ever get it finished, what with you hanging around," said Bertram rudely. "Anyway, I can't start till the moon rises tonight."

"It will be almost full tonight," said Ginny. Then she added, "Will you let me help you? You'll have to have a top for it, you know, if it's to be a rocket ship. . . . Wait! I have it." And Ginny clumped back to the sidewalk, where she skated home to return with a roll of heavy oilcloth. Meantime, Bertram had fastened on the door with leather hinges.

"Now," said Ginny, "we'll roll this oilcloth up like an ice cream cone, and fasten it to the rim of the barrel with tacks."

Now the spaceship began to look like something. "What color do you think we ought to paint it?" Ginny said.

"Red," said Bertram.

So they went to the dime store and bought a can of red paint and two brushes. At Ginny's suggestion Bertram bought some beads which, they thought, would come in handy in trading with the natives of the moon. Ginny worked on one side of the barrel while Bertram painted the other. By the time the job was finished there was almost more paint on them than on the spaceship.

As a finishing touch they painted its name, *Moon Rocket,* on opposite sides in white. They added a few peepholes in the oilcloth top, and all was ready. The spaceship looked eager to take off for the moon or even Mars or Venus.

"What are you going to take with you, besides the beads?" asked Ginny. "You'll want some ham sandwiches of course."

"And some hot dogs and pickles and jam," said Bertram.

"They say the moon's made of green cheese," said Ginny, "but I don't believe it."

"Neither do I," said Bertram, "but it will be easy enough to find out."

"But there's one thing," put in Ginny, "that we haven't thought of yet. How are you going to make it work? The spaceship, I mean. With gasoline?"

"Gasoline!" said Bertram scornfully. "As if I could take along enough gasoline to take me to the moon! Anyhow, gasoline's old-fashioned. I'm going to use atomic energy!"

"Oh!" said Ginny. "How wonderful!"

"You see," continued Bertram, "there's enough power locked up even in a little stone to pull a railroad train across the country. All you have to do is to smash an atom."

"Yes, I know," said Ginny.

As there was nothing more to be done until the moon rose, Ginny went home to change her clothes while Bertram prepared the provisions he would need. He added half a dozen candy bars.

Right after supper Bertram found Ginny waiting near the spaceship. But what neither of them knew was that while they were away, George Fish's cat, snooping around, had noticed the little door opening into the barrel, and had crawled in and gone to sleep.

It was Ginny who saw the first streak of gold bathing the hilltops.

"There it comes!" she cried. "The moon! You'd better get

in now and start smashing your atom. Have you got everything? Clean handkerchiefs? Well, good-by and good luck!"

Bertram crawled into the spaceship and fastened the little door behind him. A moment later he began banging at a pebble with a hammer. He was so busy trying to smash an atom that he never noticed George's cat. Bang! Bang! Bang!

The moon was now completely over the hilltops, shining like a big yellow Jack-o-Lantern.

Then with a *swoosh* that knocked Ginny down, Bertram's spaceship shot into the air like a skyrocket. For just one moment after she picked herself up, Ginny could see the spaceship outlined against the moon. Then it disappeared altogether.

Far up in the sky, Bertram was soaring moonward. Ginny raced along Elm Street shouting, "Bertram's gone to the moon! In his spaceship! Bertram's gone to the *moon!*"

As Ginny spread the news, the neighbors popped their heads out of windows. "Eh?" they said. "What's that? Bertram's gone to the moon? We don't believe it." And they went back to their television sets. Bertram's mama didn't believe it either. But she called down to Ginny and asked, "When?"

"Just now," said Ginny. "Didn't you hear something swoosh?"

"I heard a swoosh," said Bertram's mama, "but I thought it was Baby Sam splashing his bath water. I was giving him a bath. Did Bertram take his overshoes?"

"I wouldn't know," said Ginny. "But he did take some beads for the natives."

Then George Fish came over. And he asked Bertram's mama if she'd seen his cat.

"No, I haven't," Bertram's mama said. "For all I know, she's gone with Bertram to the moon. She's certainly not here."

"Well, he'd better bring her back," said George. "She's a very valuable cat."

Now, when Bertram hadn't come back by midnight, his mama began to worry, especially as he'd left his overshoes behind. "That boy," she said to herself, "deserves a good scolding." So she thought up the best scolding she could, and then wrote it down, so that she wouldn't possibly forget.

But where was Bertram all this time?

High up above the earth in his spaceship, soaring moonward! As he looked out through the peepholes he had cut, he could see the sky sprinkled with stars so big and bright he thought he could almost reach out and touch them. And straight ahead, the moon was getting bigger and bigger.

A shooting star whizzed past him, showering him with sparks. And something that looked like a Ferris wheel raced along with him, blazing red and green lights, then shooting off in another direction.

Bertram felt something rubbing against his legs. He looked down. George Fish's cat! How had she ever got in here, he wondered. What would George say if his cat got lost on the moon? Pussy miaowed and miaowed. But Bertram knew that if he put her out, she'd just go falling through space, and might never reach the earth. So he fed her a hot dog, and that pleased her.

Up and up and up! Right into the face of the big yellow moon. Then, suddenly Bertram felt his spaceship slipping. The atomic energy had run out! He was slipping back to earth. There wasn't a moment to lose. Another atom must be smashed if the spaceship were to get under way again. Bertram found another stone and began to hammer it. It seemed as if that atom would never get split! And the spaceship was now spinning around in a circle.

Bertram hammered with all his might. To his great relief, he felt a shock. The *Moon Rocket* was plunging on again. How silent it was there, out in space, and so cold! Even George's cat was quiet.

Bertram must have fallen asleep. He never knew how long he slept, but he wakened in a flood of light. It was hotter now, much hotter, as the spaceship neared the moon. The light was dazzling. It was like the beach on a hot midsummer's day.

The spaceship was whirling round and round. Bertram was dizzy, and the cat was clawing at his legs. Then——

PLUNK! SQUUSH!

Bertram's spaceship had come down on the moon! It bounced up more than a hundred feet, and then came down again. Once more it bounced, and kept on bouncing until it came to rest with a shudder.

Bertram crawled out, followed by the cat. He was in the middle of a hot desert surrounded by high gray mountains. There were no trees on the desert and not even any camels. No sign of life anywhere. Bertram began to wish he had never come to the moon. He thought of the folks at home, of Baby Sam and Ginny Banning and George Fish.

Then as he shaded his eyes and looked around, he saw a sign-post.

As he started to walk toward it, he felt wonderfully light on his feet. Running on ahead of him, George's cat was leaping twenty or thirty feet off the ground. Then Bertram jumped. He had never jumped so high in all his life. People back home would never believe him when he told them about this.

Now he had come to the signpost. But instead of telling him how far it was to somewhere, it read:

BATTLEGROUND
KEEP OFF!

A battleground, but with no armies in sight. Who was going to fight a battle, Bertram wondered. Suddenly George's cat pricked up her ears. A moment later, Bertram heard a sort of chirping sound. It went: Tss-Zink, Tss-Zink, Tss-Zink. Then, down one of the mountainsides swarmed something that looked at first like ants. Another swarm swept down an opposite mountainside. The Tss-zink noise grew louder.

Bertram could see now that it came from the two swarms— not of ants, but of little people. The biggest of them couldn't have been larger than a Christmas doll. Bertram gathered up the cat and hid behind a rock.

Each army was led by a chief who waved a banner. On one banner the word *TIS* was painted; on the other, the word that was painted was *TAINT*.

"Halt!" called one of the chiefs. "Halt!" barked the other. "Right face. Begin!"

What they meant to begin, Bertram, behind the rock, could not imagine. The two armies faced each other about three feet apart. When the leaders said, "Begin," the little men on one side shouted at the top of their lungs, "Tis, Tis, Tis!" while the men on the other side tried to drown them out by shouting "Taint, Taint, Taint!" Bertram listened. "Tis-taint, Tis-taint, tss-zink!" It was the same noise he had heard before the little men streamed down from the mountainside. Then, when the hubbub was loudest, the two armies began making faces, rolling their eyes, wrinkling their noses, and sticking out their tongues at each other.

Suddenly they scattered in every direction! You'd have thought a spook was after them.

But it was only George's cat. Bertram ran after it, bounding off the ground as if he wore seven-league boots and calling, "Kitty, kitty, kitty." Finally Kitty got tired and came back to Bertram.

It was quite a while before the moon men returned. They

approached timidly, the two leaders in front, each pushed by about a dozen of his followers. When they thought they were close enough, the two chiefs pointed to the cat and said, "What's that strange creature?"

"It's only a cat, you silly-billies," said Bertram. "It won't hurt you. That is, unless I tell it to." Bertram felt like a giant among these little moon men, who were all head, like polly-wogs, with skimpy little bodies and arms and legs like sticks.

"We've never seen a cat before," said the moon men. "No wonder we were scared. But who are you, and where did you come from, and why did your cat have to break up our battle? Now we won't have time to finish it."

Bertram told them his name, and added, "I came here from the earth, in my spaceship."

"The earth?" The moon men were puzzled. "Where is the earth?"

"It's down there somewhere, or up in the sky maybe. I can't see it from here. It moves around."

"Oh," said one of the moon men. "I guess you mean our moon. It comes up at night. It's big and round and bright. We write songs about it. Especially in June."

Bertram thought it odd that the earth should be somebody else's moon. The arrangement, though, seemed fair enough. "But what's all this nonsense about?" he asked. "Tis what and taint what?"

"We don't know," said the moon men. "We've forgotten. It was something that started long ago when one of our great-great-grandpas said something was so, and another said it wasn't. Then they began: 'Tis.' 'Taint.' 'Tis-taint,' like that. Until everybody took sides, the Tises on one side, the Taints on the other. Every day since then we've had our battle."

"But what good does it do?" asked Bertram, "when you don't know what's it all about, and nobody ever wins?"

"Oh, I know; I remember how it began!" It was a very old

man who had spoken up. "One of our grandpas said the moon was made of green cheese. The other said it wasn't."

"Well," said Bertram, "it's easy enough to find out. Just taste it. Does it taste like cheese?"

The moon folks wet their fingers, touched them to the ground, and put their fingers in their mouths. They shook their heads.

"No, it doesn't taste like cheese," they said. "Not a bit like cheese."

"Then," said Bertram, "you'd better all shake hands and make up." So the two chiefs shook hands and made up, and everybody smiled happily.

"Now, here are some beads," Bertram said. He divided the beads between the two leaders. And each of them gave him a silver apple marked: "Souvenir of the Moon."

"Well, I'll have to be going now," said Bertram. "Don't have any more wars."

"We won't," said the moon men. They followed him down to the spaceship and stood around it. Bertram put the cat in first, and crawled in after it. Then he began smashing an atom. It was like cracking a hickory nut. But at last it cracked, and with a *swoosh!* that bowled over the moon folks like tenpins, Bertram plunged out into space, headed earthward. Soon Bertram was out of sight.

Meanwhile, down on earth, Bertram's daddy had came home from Omaha, where he had been on business. And when he heard what Bertram had been up to, he said something must be done. So he got an astronomer to figure out just when Bertram would be back. The astronomer set down about a million figures, added them up, and then divided the answer by seven. Then he said, "Allowing two days on the moon, he should be back about nine-thirty Wednesday evening, daylight-saving time. But he will come down pretty hard, so you'd better be prepared."

Bertram's daddy telephoned the fire department and asked

the chief to have the firemen spread a life net Wednesday at nine-thirty in his back yard.

Even before eight o'clock that evening, the police roped off the yard, and the firemen stood ready with their net. A big searchlight was sweeping the sky with its beams. Neighbors came with telescopes and gazed up at the moon. A peanut wagon stood outside on the sidewalk, and a popcorn wagon too. Ginny Banning set up a lemonade stand and made a lot of money for her Bluebird group.

Nine o'clock. Nine-twenty. Nine twenty-nine! "There he comes!" shouted someone.

As the police held back the crowd, the firemen spread their net. *Zip!* Like a meteor, Bertram's spaceship plunged into the middle of the net. The spaceship bounced up as high as the old cottonwood tree. Down it came again into the net, and the firemen lowered it to the ground. The crowd gave three cheers as Bertram crawled out. His mama was so glad to see him she completely forgot the scolding she had written down. Bertram gave her the two silver apples, and she gave him a kiss. And Bertram's daddy said, "We're proud of you, my son."

Ginny had squirmed past the policemen to ask Bertram, "Was it?"

"Was it what?" said Bertram.

"Made of green cheese," said Ginny.

"No."

Then George Fish asked, "Did you bring back my cat?"

"What do you think?" said Bertram. And he opened the door of the spaceship and let George peek in. Yes, there was George's cat, curled up at the bottom of the spaceship. And with her were four of the sweetest little kittens in the world!